✝ Celtic Mythos ✝

The Obsidian Dagger

a fantasy novel

Brad A. LaMar

Dedicated to Lori, Evan, Paige, my family, and my students

&

In loving memory of my Father

+ Acknowledgments +

I would like to thank my family for supporting me in the creation of this book. They had to listen as I bounced ideas off of them and rambled on about my mythical world. I think they only thought I was partially crazy.

Lori has been the ever-supportive wife who has been there through all of the rejections with a kind word and a lot of faith in me. It is a great joy and honor to have her by my side to celebrate this success. I would like to thank my children, Evan and Paige, for always listening to my stories and encouraging me to write. Gratitude goes out to my parents who have always encouraged their son to work hard and to have faith. We miss you, Dad.

Thanks are also extended to Sara Wiley for being an awesome photographer (and taking a decent author picture of someone who isn't that photogenic) and to Rob Probus for his assistance with my author videos. Thanks also to Lauren Pfister and Wendy Eckstein for editing and offering feedback on the manuscript and to Laura Brown for proofreading the final manuscript.

Great thanks to Igor Adasikov of Taimy Studios for the fantastic artwork in the book.

I thank the readers for taking a chance on an unknown author. I only hope that you will want to come along on more adventures with me... and I do have more adventures to share.

Finally, I would like to thank Light Messages Publishing and Senior Editor Elizabeth Turnbull for her faith in my work and in the crazy world I created in Celtic Mythos. She has been a joy to collaborate with and her wisdom is valued deeply. I will forever be grateful for the opportunity to share my stories.

✛ Contents ✛

Prologue
✛ The Council of Magic ✛

IN THE CENTURIES LEADING UP to the Council of Magic, war had ravaged the Celtic Isles, tearing at the seam of reality and mysticism that bonded the two in existence. Man's reality knew very little about true magic, only scarce stories and small glimpses into that realm, leading to folklore and legend. Myths and figments stayed hidden in the shadows and were carried on whispers for generations passing from father to son and mother to daughter. The war for power grew too vast in the eyes of the council and a truce was needed.

This final meeting of the Council of Magic was recorded in the scrolls of Corways, Kingdom of the Leprechauns:

Last Meeting of the Council of Magic
Port Heggles, Scotland, August 9, 1732

In attendance:
   1) King Duncan, Leprechauns
   2) Queen Usis, Merrows
   3) King Wardicon, Sidhes
   4) Kleig, Spirit Representative (Overseer of Council of Magic)
   5) Conchar, Wizard Noble

Kleig – The meeting will now commence.

(Without much waste the others quickly quiet themselves.)

Kleig – Duncan, would you be so kind as to begin our meeting?

(Duncan rises to his feet; he remains in his Leprechaun stature.)

Duncan – Thank you, Kleig. I am very happy to see that each of our kingdoms is represented here today. As you know, our struggle for power and position has left us all in poor shape and with diminished numbers.

Usis – 'Tis true! We are driving each other to extinction.

Wardicon – Aye. But how can we resolve our squabbles in a satisfactory way?

(Conversations begin, too many and too fast for this scribe to record!)

Duncan – I am posing the idea of a treaty.

Conchar – A treaty? That is your solution?

Duncan – It is. This fighting has gotten us nowhere. Our kinds are dying and the humans are… well, the humans are advancing.

Kleig – Advancing is one way to put it.

Conchar – The humans were the reason we began fighting in the first place, lest we forget.

Usis – Their ships are ruining my waters!

Conchar – They are barbarians!

Duncan – Regardless, they are now a force in our world and it has become increasingly difficult to conceal ourselves and our battles.

Wardicon – Duncan is right. If we continue as we are, we will surely be discovered and that would mean constant harassment from the humans. None of us could withstand that for long.

Duncan – My recommendation is to go into hiding. Preserve what little we have left and live in peace.

(Conversations again break out, mumbled and stressed.)

Usis – 'Tis agreed upon by the Merrows. We choose to hide ourselves and preserve what's left of us to live in peace.

Wardicon – The Sidhe's will do the same.

Conchar – Wizards and witches have no desire to hide!

Duncan – I think you had better. Do you not remember the witch hunts and stake burnings?

Conchar – Of course I remember that injustice! Had I but been there, the human retelling would have had a much different ending.

Kleig – I don't suspect that you wish to subject your kind to that sort of tyranny again.

Conchar – No, I do not. We will live among the humans, for hiding ourselves cannot be done easily.

Kleig – Then it is decided?

(The gathered concur.)

Kleig – This is the last meeting of the Council of Magic. Our kinds will remain to themselves. The bickering ends and preservation begins. Good luck to you all.

(The Council disbands and members go their separate ways.)

✦ ✦ ✦

Conchar watched the other members of the Council vanish, fly, or spirit away before he walked to his carriage. His red-eyed doorman opened the door and lowered the step for his master. Conchar nimbly climbed in and took a seat across from his apprentice. The young witch waited patiently for her master to speak.

"The fools are giving our world over to the humans, Morna." Conchar removed his gloves with disdain on his face. "We are expected to hide amongst them, never revealing our true selves."

"Why would they agree to such stupidity?" asked the dark-eyed witch eyeing the hilt of a dagger peeking out of Conchar's cloak.

"I think they are tired of the fight." The carriage lurched to a start and slightly jostled the occupants. "It is our own fault, I suppose."

"The others are weak, master. Perhaps we should mount our own uprising. We have the means, after all."

Conchar held up his hand. "Patience, my eager apprentice." Conchar peered out through his curtains absentmindedly fingering the dagger. "Be wary of what you say, Morna. Our enemies have ways of hearing. But do not feel downtrodden, the time of retribution will come."

The carriage rolled down the worn path intent on reaching the Black Forest before first light.

Chapter 1

✛ Blue to Green ✛

BRENDAN O'NEAL WAS GLUM. He was moody. He was not enjoying himself at all. Being dragged on a trip across the entire ocean to a country where apparently there was nothing to do except watch goats eat grass and pass gas was not his idea of a good time. He could have been back home practicing with his team or working and saving up for that '81 Camaro from Newark he had seen online. Tromping half-way across the world on the wild goose chase that his father had him on was not tops on his priority list of things he wanted do in the summer before his senior year. It didn't help that his sister was sitting next to him being her normal, irritating self.

He watched her for a moment, glaring at her and the iPod that had been annoying him throughout the entire journey. She sang along to every song and she must have had a billion of them, she flailed around "dancing" in her seat occasionally knocking him upside his head. To cap it all off, she tried talking to him in the loudest voice that she had, embarrassing him and agitating everyone on board the flight.

After one final elbow to the ear, Brendan had had enough. "Lizzie, stop dancing!"

Lizzie danced on, oblivious to her brother's plea-or maybe she was just invoking her right to selective hearing.

"Lizzie, stop dancing!" he said a bit louder. When she didn't reply again, he snatched the headphones from her ears and jerked the iPod from her hand.

"Hey!" Lizzie turned to her father who was sitting across the aisle and screamed, "Dad! Brendan's trying to break my iPod !"

Oscar didn't hear the spat between his children since he had his nose buried in a thick book about Ireland. He had bought the book in the London terminal while waiting for their connecting flight to Dublin. The anthropologist was a studious person when it came to understanding culture and civilizations, but the obvious sometimes escaped his radar.

"No, I'm not!" yelled Brendan. "I just want you to stop singing and dancing. You're getting on my nerves!"

"Your face is getting on my nerves all the time," replied the spunky fifteen-year old. Her face was scrunched and her curly hair bounced as she shook her head in defiance. "Do you see me yanking on your face? No!"

Brendan furrowed his brow and held his face out. "I'd like to see you try. It'd give me a reason to toss you off this plane."

Lizzie turned back to Oscar and said, "Dad! Did you hear Brendan?"

"Hmmm?" grunted Oscar from a particularly interesting page about holiday traditions in Galway.

"He said that he was going to throw me off the plane. And he admitted that he's a big jerk."

"What? I did not!"

Oscar flipped the page and said, "That's nice."

"See, Dad just gave me permission." Brendan started to get up and grab at Lizzie's shoulders.

"Daddy!"

Oscar looked up and saw the whole ridiculous scene. "Brendan sit down and keep your hands to yourself." He watched Brendan and his glower and then added, "Please act civilized on this trip. We don't need any craziness out of you two."

"Why do we even have to go to Ireland in the first place?" complained Brendan.

"You know that it's important for my work, Brendan."

✦ ✦ ✦

A stranger watched the family with interest from three rows back. They were an odd unit with no obvious signs of power, but it was there. The stranger could sense it. This was a family that would be watched with great interest.

✦ ✦ ✦

Brendan slumped down in his seat and stewed. He was angry at his dad, and his dad knew it. High school was winding down and he had a lot of work to do. The fall was going to be his big shot at earning a soccer scholarship–– at least his coach had told him that several schools were interested in him. But, was he back in the States working on his game? No. He was stuck on a trip to exotic potato country with his brat sister and nerd father. No working out meant no scholarship, and no scholarship meant no getting away from these two.

"Look, Son, I know what you would rather be doing, but let's face it, we only have one year left as a real family. After that you'll be off to school starting your own life… it won't be the same."

"It hasn't been the same since Mom died," Brendan shot back.

"I know," Oscar agreed, pain showing behind his glasses.

"Well, I'm looking forward to this trip. Unlike some people, I think family is important," Lizzie said, narrowing her eyes at Brendan.

Brendan turned away to look out the window. "What family?" he mumbled, tossing the iPod at Lizzie.

Oscar heaved out a concerned breath. "Brendan, this trip is important to me. It's a two birds, one stone kind of trip. You know?"

Brendan rolled his eyes and replied, "I know. I know. Your research for the university and..."

"...and we're going to try and look up the old family tree. Right, Dad?" Lizzie interrupted her brother merrily.

"That's right. It's much easier to know where you are going..."

"...when you know where you've been. We've heard it before," Brendan said in disgust. Why was this whole thing so important to the old man? Who cares if the family came from here! It has little to do with my life now, he thought.

Oscar smiled wryly, "Doesn't make it any less true." Oscar leaned over and patted his son on the leg. "You'll see, son. Ireland is going to open your eyes to our past."

Brendan scoffed. "My past? I still don't know what my future will be!"

"I do," said Lizzie. "You'll be a loser."

"Shut up, Lizzie!"

Oscar interrupted the siblings. "Come on, now. There are clear skies ahead of us; let's not fight."

Lizzie glanced past Brendan at the bright blue skies that they were gliding through. "You will probably never have a girlfriend either."

Brendan thought about arguing with her but decided

to say nothing instead. The scary part was that he thought she might be right.

✦ ✦ ✦

In the churning waters of the North Channel near Islay, Aaron, and Mull, Scotland, swam the proud Queen of the Merrows. Queen Usis liked to traverse her kingdom alone when life became stressful and nearly too hard to handle.

She moved her powerful tail and cut through the water with the grace and speed of any dolphin. Her slightly graying hair trailed off her head flowing over her shoulders and into the water that she sped through. Her form was elegant and demure. She had heard many of the human sailors' tales about the beauty of the Merrows in this part of the world and the mermaids in others. Her sister, Berish, was queen in the Caribbean, married off by their father many years ago to unite the tribes.

Perhaps a visit was due, she mused. The queen knew better of the trip, though. It would be for pleasure and she had a kingdom to think of, so leaving was out of the question.

Above her head, cutting through the surface of the water rode a large vessel. Another fishing boat, no doubt. She swam to the surface, some four hundred yards off, to observe. Though her age was beginning to slow her in some areas, her vision was not affected. Neither was her voice. Once upon a time her kind would lure the foolish humans into rocks and shallow waters, but those days were gone. The humans were too numerous, and at this stage in time, they were also too advanced. All she could do this day was watch the ship from afar.

She observed as the ship cut the engine off and stopped dead in the water. A small group of men, red-eyed and deliberate in their movements, came to the side of the vessel and lowered a large net into the sea. Several things struck Queen Usis as odd. The men were few in number, to begin with, and they were dropping their net in the heat of the day. The catch would surely avoid them in favor of cooler waters and the cover of the depths.

She dropped beneath the surface to watch the net stay empty, but what she saw instead shocked her. The net broke loose of its tether and floated freely in the channel. After a moment, the net billowed out like a jellyfish. All of this was odd, but the instant the net began to move through the water in a directed path, she knew something else was afoot. Magic, perhaps?

The net's course quickly became obvious, so Usis dove as fast as her tailfin would allow her. The net narrowly missed her, but as she turned her head to find it again, she saw that it changed paths and pursued her once more.

She was a fast swimmer, but it became clear that she was no competition for the magical net. It clamped around her and encased her body in a strong fiber. The net drug her back to the fishing vessel, and the red-eyed men—though living or dead she could not say for certain—pulled her aboard and packed her away in a thick glass container. No words were exchanged. No violence was enacted, only the box and a lid, and then darkness as they stored her in the cargo hold like the catch of the day.

✦ ✦ ✦

The airplane had made a nice, steady, and smooth landing in the Dublin Airport and had taxied to a stop near Terminal D. All of the passengers gathered their belongings after they were told that it was safe to do so, and began filing off the plane. Lizzie, Oscar, and Brendan were the last ones off. They stood in the plane's doorframe as a family and soaked in the sun.

"Feels good, doesn't it?" Oscar said with a huge smile on his face.

"Uh-huh," replied Brendan, pulling on his shades. "This airport is tiny. I thought Dublin was supposed to be some big city here."

"It is, idiot," began Lizzie. "If you would have looked at the website that Dad told us about you would see that this isn't a transcontinental airport. It doesn't need to be big."

"Whatever, Liz," Brendan groaned.

"What'd I tell you, kids? Clear skies." Oscar sucked in another long breath of fresh air. "It look's like it's going to be a great start to our trip after all."

Almost instantly, the clouds covered the sun and dumped hundreds of thousands of gallons of water from the sky. Lizzie pulled her hood up and sprinted down the steps and towards the terminal.

Brendan pulled his hat a little lower and said, "Yup. You called it, Dad. Clear skies."

Oscar shook his head and watched his son bound down the steps. After a small sigh, he followed.

✦ ✦ ✦

The dark stranger emerged from the plane and continued to watch the family. He took the steps, not in any kind of a hurry, and followed the rest of the passengers into the terminal.

✦ ✦ ✦

Oscar came through the double glass doors and spotted his children shaking off the droplets of water. Most of the passengers on the small connecting flight were walking a short distance to the baggage carousal.

Grumpy and damp passengers congregated around the circular cone that the Dublin airport used. The bags shot out of a window that was fed by a conveyor belt and then slid down to the cone to the waiting travelers. Their baggage had yet to come down and people around them didn't seem to be in patient moods.

"Great. No bags yet," grumbled a large man with a thick Scottish accent. The big Scotsman grabbed a rail-thin airport worker by the arm as the young man was strolling by and said, "Hey, when are they going to get our bags off the plane?"

To his credit, the skeletal airport employee didn't show any signs of intimidation and jerked his arm free before he answered. "They'll get it when they get it, now won't they?"

"Bah!" retorted the Scot.

Brendan smiled at the encounter as the employee continued his stroll, apparently unaffected, to join his buddies standing near a cute blonde that manned the gate.

"Dad, who knows when these yahoos are going to get our bags off," observed Lizzie.

As if on queue, the skinny employee started jumping around and making donkey noises in the midst of his conversation. His buddies laughed, but the passengers only grumbled.

"We could be here for hours," Lizzie continued.

"Well, then that's going to give me time to go and get the rental car." Oscar patted Brendan on the shoulder and said, "I'll probably need some help driving on this trip, Son."

Brendan's eyes lit up. "You serious?"

"Sure," smiled Oscar. "That's, of course, if you can handle the power of the vehicle they give me. I already put you down as a second driver."

"Sweet!"

"You guys hang out here and get the bags. I'll meet you at the pick-up gate in twenty minutes." Oscar walked away studying the printout he had of the car rental company's confirmation email.

Lizzie and Brendan walked over to the baggage carousal once sounds could be heard from the conveyor window. Moments later, a few bags began to plop out and land at the bottom of the cone. A few people scurried up to grab their bags, including the big Scot. He ambled up, and just as he took his bag by the handle, a large golf bag tumbled down and smashed him in the face.

"Whoa! Did you see that?" laughed Lizzie.

"What in the bloody hell was that?" The Scot bellowed toward the crowd of workers.

The thin employee strolled over to the big man. "Is there a problem here?"

"You bet there is," huffed the Scot. "I got hit in the face by a bloody golf bag!" The large man's eyes were small in his pillowy cheeks but they were intense and fixed on the young airport worker.

"Well, sir, just maybe you should have moved your big, fat face out of the way."

The Scot's face grew to a bright red and a low growl rumbled in his throat. Brendan looked on with the rest of the crowd and waited for the large guy to either choke the thin guy or blow his top like a volcano.

"You rude, little son of a…" the large Scot began to move toward the worker when an alarm with a rotating yellow light burst to life above the conveyor window. The worker and the Scot glanced up at the window and saw that there was a luggage backup.

"Don't worry, folks. I've got this," boasted the young worker. He began climbing over bags that already sat upon the cone, not being cautious or overly concerned about smashing the contents until he reached the window. "Why do you always have to do this, Bessie? You're making me look bad."

The big Scot glowered at the young man while everyone else just exchanged curious glances. The worker began tugging on different bags, trying to loosen the logjam.

"Come on! I've got you now!" he exclaimed as he pulled as hard as he could.

The bags came loose and an avalanche of luggage spewed from the window. The massive flow swept the worker up and threw him backwards down the carousal. Somewhere in the fray the young skinny guy was thrown aside as the rest of the bags crashed full force into the big Scot. People walked over and plucked their bags off of the big man one at a time. Lizzie had to get hers from the carousal. It happened to be one on the worker's face as he traveled around and around on the cone.

"Uh... thanks," she said as she lifted her bag off. "Found it!" she yelled over to Brendan.

Brendan collected his and his father's bags and they made their way to the pick-up gate leaving a very strange scene behind them. If this was any indication of what it was going to be like in Ireland, Brendan and Lizzie were preparing themselves for a really weird vacation.

Brendan and Lizzie walked through the pick-up gate and set the bags off to the side. The pick-up gate was no more than a covered throughway where cars could pick-up passengers. There was a paved road that stretched in both directions. The storm was past, but there was still a drizzle that made it hard to see what surrounded the airport. Haze and mist were floating in the air and a ton of puddles mirrored the haze. It was an ominous view no matter where they looked.

Brendan sat down on his bag and noticed that they

seemed to be the only people getting picked up at the supposed pick-up gate. "This must not be a popular spot. It's so empty."

Lizzie nodded. "It's sort of creepy. I feel like we're in a big cemetery."

Brendan couldn't argue with that.

"How long did Dad say?"

Brendan glanced at the time on his cell phone and said, "Twenty minutes."

"How long has it been?"

"About an hour," responded Brendan.

A low rumbling sounded from the distance and the O'Neal kids looked up the road. Two headlight beams were cutting through the haze. As it came a little closer, they could see a red Ferrari speeding down the road in their direction.

"Man, about time. Awesome car, though." Brendan was imagining himself at the wheel feeling like a superstar. How sweet was that going to be!

"Maybe Dad will let me drive, too," said Lizzie.

"Keep dreaming," Brendan scoffed. "Dad's never going to let you drive."

"He'll let me drive before he lets you," she sassed back.

Brendan rolled his eyes. "You don't know what you're talking about."

The Ferrari sped closer and showed no signs of slowing. The kids stepped back away from the road and leaned against the building. The car blasted through the pick-up gate splashing water all over them and in the process created such a vortex of wind that they were nearly knocked off their feet. Brendan wiped water from his eyes and looked over at his sister. Her curly locks were soaked and hung sadly in her face. He reached over and plucked a leaf out of her hair.

As they stood dripping, Oscar pulled under the awning in a very small, very European hatchback. It was tiny and sputtered. Black smoke choked out of the tailpipe and filled the air around them. The paint was spotty at best as the metal shone fully in several places, at least it did where the rust hadn't already taken over.

Oscar popped out of the driver seat and slapped the top of the car. "Load her up, kids."

Brendan and Lizzie stood frozen in place, sopping wet and shocked. Oscar apparently did not notice the glazed expressions and lack of movement and strolled over and placed an arm around his kids' shoulders.

"She's a beaut, huh? Soak it in. That is a European classic." He slapped Brendan on the back and continued, "And the best part is, you'll get to drive her around most of the time. I mean, I'll be busy with my research, so you'll get to have a little time to cruise. Hey, watch out Irish girls… eh?"

Oscar grabbed his bag and went to the trunk. Lizzie moved in closer to her brother. "Yeah, watch out girls, because the fumes may kill you." She grabbed her bag and loaded it into the small space.

"Let's go, Brendan. We're burning daylight," called Oscar.

Brendan loaded his bag as his mind flashed warnings of how lame this whole trip was really going to be. He only coughed seven or eight times on the fumes.

The dark stranger stood in the rain pondering his next move. It had become clear that this family had been what he was waiting on for centuries. All he needed to do now was to "get the ball rolling," as the Americans would say.

Chapter 2

+ Galway or Bust +

The O'Neal's new-to-them car bobbed wearily through the countryside outside of Dublin. Brendan watched the pretty scenery crawl by his window since the beater his dad rented could barely outrun a slow lawn mower or a fast sloth.

Brendan leaned on his arm rest and chewed on his

fingernail. "Where are we going, Dad?"

"Galway," replied Oscar. He merrily drummed his fingers on the steering wheel, an old habit that he had since before his band broke up in college.

"Why Galway?" Lizzie asked loudly from the back seat, headphones firmly in place.

Oscar smiled. "That's supposed to be where it all began." The static-filled signal on the AM radio crackled to life and Oscar was quick to turn the volume dial up. "Alright! Sing with me. Danny boy, Danny boy, the tides, the tides are calling." Noticing that he was alone in song, he looked at his kids.

"Are you listening? Darn iPods."

Smoke poured out from the exhaust pipe leaving a nice trail behind the O'Neals as they putted down the country roads. Brendan absently studied an Irish road map, Lizzie slumbered in the backseat, and Oscar peered through his reading glasses, which were balanced precariously on the end of his nose, at a printed sheet of directions while he drove.

"When we get there, Brendan, we need to head straight up to the room and get settled in."

Brendan nodded. "Is this a hotel?"

Oscar raised a brow to consider the comparison. "It's more like a bed and breakfast. We may have the whole thing to ourselves, though. I don't think this is a peak travel season."

Oscar handed the printout of the directions over to Brendan and he saw that it was folded and stapled. He flipped it to the front page and saw several images that Oscar had printed off of the hotel. Galway looked kind of cool. It didn't seem like an isolated farm town or anything like that, so perhaps the trip could be okay. There were a few pictures of a castle and something that resembled civilization.

Galway was just like the pictures had promised, but to Brendan, the place looked a whole lot smaller. They found the bed and breakfast right away. It was a modest three-story home on the end of a narrow cobblestone street. A sign above the porch read "Gordy's Home" and beneath the sign, rocking in their chairs, sat an elderly couple.

Oscar pulled the car to a stop in front of the place. The car threw out a loud *Bang* and a puff of exhaust. Luckily no one was around or Brendan would have been really embarrassed. He looked at the old guy in his blue jeans and white-buttoned down shirt and the old lady with her flower-patterned dress and hair up in a bun and heaved out a short breath.

"Gordy, you think?"

Oscar opened his door and said, "Probably. Stay here and I'll make sure." He got out and approached the old couple.

Brendan looked back at his sister. She was slumped against the window with a small line of slobber stringing out of the corner of her mouth.

"Wake up, Liz. We're here."

Lizzie sort of woke up. "Huh? Here?" She rubbed her eyes and saw that her dad was coming back to the car.

"Is that Gordy?" asked Brendan.

"Sure is and he told me to park around back." Oscar walked around to the trunk. "Pop the hatch for me, will ya?"

Brendan leaned over and complied. He opened his own door and got out to stretch his legs. Lizzie emerged from the backseat, iPod humming.

"Lizzie, help your old dad with the bags while Brendan parks the car."

Brendan cracked his neck to relieve some tension in his shoulders and walked over to the driver seat. "How do I get to the back?"

Oscar handed a bag to Lizzie, who promptly put it on the ground and shuffled her songs. "Gordy said that there was some alley just down the street. Turn right there, get to the end of the buildings, and turn right again. You'll see Gordy's lot from there."

Oscar cleared the trunk and then closed it. He and Lizzie began lugging the luggage to the front door. Gordy almost got up to help.

Almost.

Brendan drove very slowly down the street passing many homey buildings all housing varying businesses. There was a restaurant, a clothing shop (with the coolest styles no doubt), a souvenir shop, a bookstore, a pub, and a gas station.

"Food, clothes, junk, books. Oh a bar… whoa! Look at that guy," Brendan said aloud to an empty car.

A fifty-something guy was stumbling around on the

sidewalk with a woman under his arm. They were talking loudly, but Brendan wasn't in earshot at the time. The man stopped walking and broke into an Irish jig. As he drove a little further, Brendan caught a snippet of their conversation.

"Look at me," slurred the man. "I'm dancing a jig!"

The woman frowned and crossed her arms. "Would you cut that out? You're not even Irish."

The man paused in mid-jig and looked her square in the eye. "Well, I should have been." The guy jumped back into his jig, dancing circles around the woman. Brendan drove on.

"Ah, the alley," declared Brendan. He turned the car and half-blocked the sidewalk. He stopped well short of the alley's entrance and stared at the ultra-narrow path between the buildings. "How am I supposed to fit down there?"

The man and the woman stumbled in front of Brendan's car and paused. The guy looked at the alley and then back at Brendan's car. After taking a few looks back and forth, the man hollered out, "I wouldn't even try that and I'm three sheets to the wind."

The woman grabbed the guy by the arm and dragged him down the sidewalk. Brendan waited for them to get out of the way before sticking his head out of the window to reexamine the problem.

"There's no way."

"You can make it, you chicken," taunted an Irish-accented voice from the left.

"You must be crazy," Brendan responded and looked over to the owner of the voice. She was beautiful, like an angel. Was that harp music? He shook it off and tried to play it a little cooler. "Have you been in that pub, too? There's no way I can make it through there."

The girl chuckled and then walked over and opened the door. "Slide over, chicken. Let a woman show you how it's done." She shoved Brendan into the passenger seat, slammed the door shut, popped the clutch, and jammed on the accelerator.

Brendan braced himself against the dash and the door, and watched as the walls of the buildings that lined the alley went streaking by like they were going into light speed. The mirrors were no more than a half-inch from scrapping along the walls! Brendan cringed and gritted his teeth as they shot out of the alley and whipped a hard right. They peeled out and drifted until the tires gripped the surface of the road. They blazed a path down the road until they reached Gordy's lot and the girl pulled a sharp left. The car began to spin out of control until it came to rest in between a pair of rusted out trucks.

"Now that was some fun," laughed the girl. "I'm Dorian, by the way. You got a name of your own, or should I keep calling you chicken?"

Brendan peeled his hands free of their grips and looked at the angel who drove like the devil. "My name's Brendan."

"Oh, a Yank, eh?" She sized him up for a moment. "It's nice to meet you, Brendan." She threw her door open and stepped out. She started to strut away.

Brendan jumped out of the passenger side and shouted, "Wait up!" He hustled over to where she was standing. "Wait. Where are you going?"

Dorian playfully swiped a lock of auburn hair out of her face, only to allow it to fall back down again. She smiled and bit her lower lip, clearly showing some sort of interest in Brendan. "I must be off for home, Brendan the Yank. It's getting late, and a lady can't be too careful."

"Something tells me that you can handle yourself. Like that driving! That was amazing! Where did you learn to drive like that?"

Dorian smiled a little broader. "I've got a confession. That was my first time behind the wheel." She reveled in Brendan's shocked look. "It sure was fun though."

He continued to stare, and his mouth opened up without his control.

"With your mouth open like that you remind me of my Uncle Colym after a late night." Dorian glanced into the darkening sky. "I've really got to be moving on now."

As she began to walk away, Brendan called after her. "When can I see you again?"

She stopped and glanced back over her shoulder, melting Brendan where he stood. She treated him with one last dazzling smile before disappearing into the shadows.

✦ ✦ ✦

"Hey, Gordy," Brendan said, entering through the front porch. "And Mrs. Gordy," he added, spying the elderly lady smoking an ancient pipe.

He took the stairs two at a time, the vision of her smile fresh in his mind. He went all the way to the third floor and came to a door that said "Suite." He knocked and Lizzie snapped her gum as she let him into the living space.

He took stock of what the living conditions were going to be like for the foreseeable future and his disposition slumped. It was a very small suite, if that's what it could be called. He was standing in the living room in which an old worn-out couch was the centerpiece. A small kitchenette was near the window that overlooked the lot. The piece de résistance was the sweet twenty-seven inch boxy television sitting on a wobbly end table. Was this the Hilton?

"This is it? This is the great place you rented?" Brendan asked Oscar who was taking in Galway from the window.

"Yup." The scientist exhaled a breathe of satisfaction. "Isn't it great? A little piece of Ireland. You know?"

Brendan and Lizzie exchanged looks. "It's a little smaller than I expected."

"And there are only two bedrooms," added Lizzie.

Brendan turned back to his father. "Yeah, how about the sleeping arrangements?"

Lizzie walked over and put a hand on his shoulder. "Brendan, it's the comfy couch for you, bub." She followed that bit of good news with a hearty, aggravating laugh.

"What?" Brendan said incredulously. "Who decided that?"

"We did when you were out there flirting with that girl.

As if you had a chance." Lizzie grinned a demon's smile and popped her gum a couple of times.

Oscar stepped in before Brendan could respond. "Well, you are going to get to drive the car a lot, so I had to give Lizzie something."

"Besides," Lizzie said. "I called dibs."

"You can't do that!"

Lizzie skipped to her bedroom door, very pleased with herself and said, "Can and did." She shut the door behind her leaving Brendan smoldering.

"Dad, come on now. You don't think I can sleep on that couch, do you?"

Oscar nodded his understanding. "Son, you don't have to sleep on that couch."

Relief swept over Brendan. "Thank you."

"I mean, the floor looks pretty comfortable, too. Good night, Son." Oscar stepped into his own room and closed the door.

Brendan couldn't believe his terrible luck. He flopped back onto the couch to test its comfort level. The thin upholstery barely hid the springs beneath and when he moved a couple of sharp ends stabbed at his back. One spring tore through and flew across the room.

"Great," huffed Brendan. "Let's see what's on." He found the remote in the cracks of the cushions and pressed the "On" button. The TV sputtered like the rental car and then popped. Smoke came out of somewhere in the back. All Brendan could do was sigh.

Chapter 3
✦ Learninig the Legend ✦

*I*T'S THE WORLD CUP FINAL *and Brendan O'Neal is lined up to take the last shot on goal in Sudden Death. The throngs of fans in Rio de Janeiro sing and cheer as they wait for the two-time scoring champion from New York City to strike. Drumming and shakers resonate throughout the stadium, and Brendan smiles to himself. He has already* kicked it past this goalie three times this game. The next one is going to be cake.

Brendan wipes a bead of sweat from his brow and looks around the stands, soaking in the moment. Fans from all around the world are cheering him on, but that is to be expected. He was, after all, the most popular player on the planet. O'Neal is the new bar upon which all the others are measured and he sure sets the bar high. There are so many movie stars and celebrities in the crowd on this night, but they are all there to see him. Then he spots her. Dorian is there in the crowd, in red, white, and blue, rooting for him even though he was just about to defeat the pesky Irish football team.

He gives her a head nod for a little acknowledgement and then he focuses back on the goal. He considers his options and then charges forward. He plants his left foot and draws his right leg back as his muscles ripple and cameras flash. Dorian begins to smile and her dazzling white teeth begin to glow. They glow brighter and brighter until they approach the sun's intensity. Brendan loses track of where the ball is, but it's too late to stop the forward motion of his foot. He barely clips the top part of the ball and it weakly rolls to the feet of the goalie. Brendan lays on the ground, blinded and humiliated. He raises his arm to shield his eyes from the glare.

✦ ✦ ✦

"Top o' the morning to you," Oscar mused after throwing the curtains back and exposing the living room to a flood of light.

Brendan's head was flopped back on top of the couch cushion with his rear planted numbly on the stained carpet. He began to stir and raise his arm to block the light.

"Huh? Sun... too bright!" he chortled like Frankenstein's monster.

"I know, I know. Keep it down," Oscar said moving over to sit beside Brendan. "Lizzie's still sleeping."

Brendan opened one weary eye towards his father and said, "Why am I awake?"

"I'm heading into town. I'm going to their records building and then I'm going to talk to some of the locals." Brendan struggled to pull himself up to the couch. Oscar continued. "Go sleep in my bed for awhile, but when you get up don't forget to get Lizzie up and take her with you. I've left some money on the table."

Brendan glanced over and saw the bills and then he got to his feet. Oscar led him to the bedroom doorway.

"Have a nice day," Oscar slipped away and out the door.

Brendan wobbled where he stood and then fell over into the bedroom. Unfortunately, the bed was on the other side of the room.

✦ ✦ ✦

Hours later, closer to the time where normal people start their day, Lizzie and Brendan stepped onto the front porch and found themselves in the company of Gordy and Mrs. Gordy. They were once again rocking their lives away in their chairs. Brendan guessed that they too had started the day way too early.

"So, Brendan, where are we going?" asked Lizzie.

"There are a bunch of places down the street, Liz. I

thought we could go down there today and then maybe drive around later."

Lizzie shrugged. "Whatever, as long as we eat."

"If you would have been up at a decent hour you could have had some of my home-cooked breakfast, now couldn't you?" chimed in Mrs. Gordy.

Brendan was taken aback by the old lady's shrewdness. "Oh, sorry we missed that. I guess we'll have to eat at the restaurant next door."

Gordy snickered a little. "I don't think you will. You see, that place has been closed for awhile now."

"You can go to the pub, though," offered Mrs. Gordy.

"The pub?" asked Lizzie.

Brendan cut in and said, "We're not old enough to go in there."

Gordy assured Brendan that dining in there was perfectly legal. Brendan was adamant about being right with the law since he had heard such horrible things about foreign jails. He wasn't sure what crimes would lead to what sentences here, so better safe than sorry.

"Just be mindful of Finnagan," warned Mrs. Gordy. "He gets to talking when he's had his fill, he does."

Brendan and Lizzie thanked Gordy and Mrs. Gordy and began to walk down the street towards the pub.

It took a moment for their eyes to adjust to the dim lighting in Ewen's Pub. Brendan and Lizzie stood in the doorway a moment and listened to the chatter subside and silence replace it. Brendan didn't have to see the faces in the pub to know where everyone was looking. They stepped inside and got a better look at the interior of the place and its patrons.

Lizzie was struck by all the characters in the bar and became a little hesitant. She thought they looked like muggers and vagrants. "Maybe this wasn't a good idea."

Brendan smiled and leaned down to whisper, "I think it will be fine, Liz." He lead her forward to the bar where a forty-something barkeep was polishing a mug.

"Welcome to Ewen's. Come have a seat at the bar," the barkeep said smiling broadly, gesturing towards a couple of stools. He looked nice enough, so the O'Neal kids did as he suggested.

"My name's Ewen. What can I get you?"

Lizzie smiled back at the nice man. "What do you have, Ewen?"

Brendan shot his sister a look. "Lizzie, don't be rude."

"She's right, lad. I haven't told you what we have, now have I?" Ewen bent down and started digging around in boxes beneath the counter. He mumbled to himself and made a lot of racket. "Now where did I put those menus?"

A waitress got to the bar at about that time and scoffed. "Menus? When did this place have menus?" She winked at the kids and started unloading her tray on the bar top.

Ewen stood up and looked offended. "Come now, Molly, this is a respectable establishment."

"Respectable? Ha!" Molly howled. She left with her empty tray.

The man on Brendan's right leaned forward over the bar to address the kids. "Where did you say you were from?" This man was grizzly and was badly in need of a shave.

Brendan felt uncomfortable and cleared his throat. "We didn't."

"They sound American to me," a fat man at a table nearby called out.

"Right, right," added his drinking buddy. "What brings you all this way?"

"Our father is doing some research and trying to look up some family history," answered Lizzie cheerfully.

Brendan couldn't believe his ears. Had she never heard about not talking to strangers? "Lizzie!"

Ewen jumped up from behind the bar with some aged menus in hand. "Ah-hah! My menus."

Molly returned to the bar, tray filled with empty pints and plates. "Menus? Looks more like napkins to me." She glanced at the kids and winked. "Maybe even toilet paper."

The grizzly guy was still keen to learn more about the new comers and continued to press. "What's your last name then?"

Fat man chomped on a fried something and added through sprays of food. "Yeah, we may know some of your relatives."

Brendan looked back to Lizzie. "Don't. We don't know these people."

Drinking buddy raised a glass. "This isn't America, sonny. Everyone knows everyone here."

Lizzie was satisfied with that answer. "Our last name is O'Neal." She smirked at Brendan who was squirming on his barstool.

The pub fell dead silent for the second time since they had walked in only this time a collective gasp preceded the quiet. All the heads in the room turned to the back corner, which was covered in shadow. The only light came from the end of a lit pipe that had a thin trail of smoke floating up and away from it.

"O'Neal, is it?" came the gruff voice from the corner. The man emerged from the shadow with his pipe clutched in his teeth. His long coat hung large on his shoulders. "Oh, I can tell you about the clan O'Neal."

The man stepped forward amidst the silence, his heels click-clacking on the wood floor. His eyes were wild and he was beginning to frighten the O'Neal kids. He stared at the kids and then stopped his march. "We are talking O-N-E-A-L, right?"

Lizzie nodded.

"Lizzie!" Brendan admonished.

"Sorry, I can't stop myself," she replied.

"It's a sad tale, it is. I hate to be the one who has to inform you," said the man.

Molly was standing near the bar rolling her eyes. "No you're not, Finnagan. You love this story."

"Fine then. Let me tell it." Finnagan cleared his throat like a master storyteller preparing to amaze his audience. "Many moons ago, the O'Neal clan founded a nearby town that they named Corways. I can't remember why, but they did. Anyhow, several other clans joined them and they were living a right fine life."

"All was well, it was," added the drinking buddy.

"Then the strangest thing happened," said Finnagan.

"Odd it was. All the townspeople disappeared," interrupted grizzly.

Finnagan gave him a look and then continued. "No one knew what happened to these poor, poor people." Finnagan paused for dramatic affect.

Drinking buddy leaned forward and whispered, "Magic. That's my guess."

"Yes, magic," spat Finnagan, now getting a little frustrated by all of the interruptions. "Since the cursed souls of Corways vanished, the town has remained empty."

"Dead to the world," added the fat guy.

"Now, there have been folks, sober folks at that, who've gone there and brought back all sorts of amazing stories."

Lizzie, now getting into the tale asked, "Like what?"

Finnagan smiled, happy to have control of the story again. "Most come back spooked by noises or claims of seeing things in the greenery, but many have come back with even more amazing claims that make us question their sanity."

"Or their sobriety," quipped Molly.

"What did they see?" Lizzie asked eagerly.

"Well, when an Irish storm hits, the wind howls and the rain beats down drowning our beautiful land..."

"Seen it," grumbled Brendan.

"...But on few occasions, a ray of hope breaks through the clouds and lets us know that God's still watching."

"A rainbow, he means," clarified drinking buddy.

"Yes, a rainbow, you daft twit. Of course they knew I was talking about a rainbow, for heaven's sake." Finnagan composed himself and continued. "It touches down in the middle of Corways and something magical happens."

Now it was Brendan's turn to interrupt. "Let me guess—there are little Leprechauns running around in green hats and suits with beards and a big pot of gold ripe for the taking. That about right?"

Molly sent him a quizzical look. "Are you sure you're not from around here?"

"It's true!" hollered Finnagan. "I've seen it with my own eyes. Little people in green, dancing around catching light."

Grizzly nodded his confirmation. "The truth, he tells."

Brendan looked the guy in the eye. "You've seen it too?"

Grizzly considered it and then said, "Well, no, but he tells the story so convincingly."

Brendan chuckled. "Well, thanks for the story."

Ewen placed two plates in front of the O'Neals. "I knew he would go on and on about that, so I fetched you the day's special."

Brendan eyed Finnagan as he returned to his dark corner, pipe still burning and bouts of coughing overtaking his mumblings. "Leprechauns," he scoffed. "Doesn't that guy know that smoking will kill him?"

Lizzie put her mouth close to Brendan's ear and whispered, "Do you think our ancestors were really

Leprechauns?"

"Sure. It might explain why you're so short."

Lizzie's eyes widened in absolute shock. "What?"

He just shook his head. "Just eat your food."

✦ ✦ ✦

The patrons of Ewen's Pub were so enraptured with the tale and the interaction with visitors that none of them noticed his arrival. Normally people would shudder and immediately move away from him, but not on this occasion. The dark stranger had slipped into the pub unnoticed and watched the entire scene. The crazy man's tale had confirmed his suspicions about the family and he smiled a rare smile. The time had finally arrived and the O'Neal's homecoming was the sign that he had been waiting for.

✦ ✦ ✦

An hour later the O'Neal kids emerged from Ewen's Pub. The food was a traditional Irish meal that neither one could remember the name of, but both found to be less than tasty. They ate the dishes out of politeness. They were not going to add to the rude-American image.

"What I wouldn't give for some chicken fingers," commented Lizzie.

"I would have just taken chicken anything." Brendan looked down the street at the gas station and frowned. "There's that Ferrari that splashed us. Let's go let the air out of his tires."

"Yeah," grinned Lizzie.

They began walking that direction, but froze when

they saw a behemoth, bodybuilder-type guy with a puffy blonde mullet arrogantly strut out to the driver's side. He had a beef jerky stick in his mouth and a bottle of water in his hand.

"Whoa," said Brendan pulling up short. "That is one big dude."

"Yeah, but let's take him down anyway." Lizzie caught Brendan's look of panic and added, "What? He's eating beef jerky and I am starving for something American."

As the Ferrari peeled out and disappeared from sight, Brendan turned back towards Gordy's Place. "Let's go."

Lizzie followed, a forelorned look on her face. "Hey, you don't think those stories we heard were true, do you?"

"No, they're just stories. They're probably just trying to freak us out."

Brendan walked on and Lizzie lumbered behind, the thought of beef jerky dancing through her mind.

✦ ✦ ✦

"Evening, kids," greeted Oscar as he burst through the door to the living room. He looked expectantly at his children who were too engrossed in their iPods and cell phones to notice him. "Did you have a nice day?"

"It was great," said Brendan sarcastically. "We walked around for about an hour and saw the entire town. Shocker, huh?" He held a smug look on his face for a beat or two and then returned to texting his friends.

"We did get to go in a pub today," interjected Lizzie with zeal.

"A what? A pub?" Oscar looked disapprovingly at

Brendan. "Come on, Brendan. A pub? You should know better than that."

"It was fine. There's no rule against it," sighed Brendan. Seeing that his father was backing down from the high horse for a moment he added, "Oh, and you can stop all the research now because we know what happened to our ancestors."

"Really?" Oscar waited patiently expecting to be entertained by this tale.

"Tell him, Liz."

Lizzie put her iPod down and adjusted her position in her seat. "Well, there was this weird Irish guy with a real crazy accent who got all creepy and started telling us that the O'Neal clan were a bunch of Leprechauns from Corways."

"Uh-huh," said Oscar with a goofy grin like someone was trying to pull a fast one on him.

"That's what he said."

"That's right, Dad. Leprechauns." Brendan smiled broadly at his dad. "Now that the mystery is solved, can we please go home?"

Oscar began to pour himself a drink in the kitchenette and he chuckled. "As solid as that sounds, I think we'll go ahead and stay. Not that the weird Irish guy isn't a credible source and all, but I think I'll look for more substantial leads in the records."

Brendan heaved out the sigh of an anguished teen and Lizzie ignored him. "Hey, Dad, while you're doing your thing, do you care if we check out Corways? It's really not that far from here."

"Mmmmm, I'm not sure." Looking at Lizzie, he saw the familiar puppy dog eyes she often employed to get her way. "Okay, if it's not that far and you have a cell phone on you at all times."

"It probably doesn't exist anyway, Dad," Brendan said giving a doubtful gaze in Lizzie's direction.

"Yes, it does," Lizzie spoke with a clear confidence. "I can feel it."

Brendan laughed. "Is your Leprechaun sense tingling?"

Lizzie folded her arms and replied with the always witty, "Shut up." Though she wasn't sure if it was Leprechaun sense or hunger pangs.

The scenery in Ireland was green, fresh, simple, and in many ways, breathtaking. Wardicon always felt that way. Even as a young Sidhe, he found out quickly that he was one who enjoyed nature. His mother, the former queen of the Sidhes, had instilled in him a love and appreciation for their home.

He liked to sit near the top of an old tree that was just on the edge of his forest and watch the stars and the moon move across the sky. He liked to imagine how large the universe was beyond what he could see and many a night he would get so caught up in his thoughts that everything else around him faded out of his mind. It was consuming and in some ways very dangerous.

He was so lost in his imagination and ponderings that he failed to see the large human-like figure approach from the road. He failed to see the being lift his arm with a gleaming hatchet in hand and fling it through the air. It was too late to do anything by the time he realized that his branch had been cut from the tree. Despite the fact that he had wings he wasn't going to be able to catch himself before he hit the ground. By mercy or command, the large figure snatched him from the air and rudely shoved him into a burlap sack. Darkness surrounded him along with a distinct odor that he could not place. His mind couldn't think on it long since he was rendered unconscious and taken away from his starry night.

Chapter 4
✢ Rainbow Hunting ✢

BRENDAN WAS HALF AWAKE when Oscar ventured into the living room from his bedroom. He heard his old man shuffling here and there gathering papers and books, opening the curtains and mumbling about the overcast skies, and making a little noise in the kitchenette. Soon enough the coffee maker was percolating and the fresh blended smell of Columbian coffee beans wafted through the air almost enticing him to get up and join his dad for a cup. Instead, Brendan got to his feet and stumbled into his father's room, and shut the door behind him.

Oscar turned when he heard the door close and saw that the couch was now vacant. "Well, good morning to you, too," he mused. Oscar bundled up his briefcase, threw an umbrella under his arm, and grabbed his coffee and left the suite.

Brendan settled himself into the lumpy bed and found just the right position. He was slowly drifting off to sleep when a crash of thunder boomed in the distance and an excited screech boomed from somewhere much closer.

"No," groaned Brendan, forcing his eyes shut. "Go back to bed, Lizzie," he mumbled to his empty room. He was hoping that he wouldn't have to yell at her. He needed to cash in on some much needed sleep.

"Brendan!" yelled Lizzie from the living room. "Where are you?"

Brendan heard her and imagined that she was digging through his blankets on the couch.

"Brendan!" she hollered again.

"What?" he slurred through his sleepiness, but she kept yelling for him, so he mummy-walked to the door and slung it open intent on blowing up on her.

Thud! went the door and Ouch! went Lizzie.

"Uh, Lizzie?" Brendan looked around the door and grimaced. He held out his hand and helped her to her feet. "Are you okay?"

To her credit, she only briefly rubbed her head and then said, "I'm fine. Did you see that it's raining?" She smiled like someone who hadn't just taken a door to her face.

Brendan lifted an eyebrow. "Yeah. So?"

She looked at him incredulously. "So? So, rain can bring rainbows. Duh."

"You've got to be kidding me," he laughed. He was so tired that he thought the whole scene was ludicrous. "You think that I'm going to drive you out to the middle of nowhere in search of a rainbow in this storm?" He waited for her to show some recognition of how asinine the idea was, but when she just smiled wider, he could only shake his head.

"You must be crazy."

✦ ✦ ✦

"I hate you. You know that, right?" Brendan said half-seriously. He adjusted the windshield wipers to the fastest setting, which happened to be slow and choppy. The road was bumpy and saturated and the old car plodded along at a snail's pace.

"No, you don't. You love me." Lizzie smiled the devil's smile at her big brother. "Are you sure this is the right way?"

"This is the way Gordy told me to go." Brendan thought back to the conversation and laughed. Gordy was rocking back and forth and came to a sudden stop when Brendan asked about Corways. The old man told them to not waste their time and blah, blah, blah, but Brendan stopped listening. What did old people know?

"I just don't want to get lost."

Brendan made a *humph* sound. "I have my cell phone, and besides, this was your idea. You were the one wanting to go rainbow hunting."

"I know," she sassed. "I get it."

"Just keep an eye out for the rainbow," Brendan commanded.

"Will do, Captain," Lizzie said with a salute.

They drove on for a ways in silence. Brendan looked out through the water-soaked windshield and worked hard to keep the car on the road.

"I can't believe that I'm rainbow hunting," he laughed with a small bit of hysteria. "I can just hear it when we get home. 'How was your trip to Ireland, Brendan?' And I'll say, 'It was swell. We looked for rainbows all day long, and then we found one and then we rode bareback on a unicorn.' They are all going to think I'm crazy!"

Lizzie watched his rant. "So, you think this is a waste of time, huh?"

He looked her in the eye. "I do. Oh, and if anyone back home asks, we did not go rainbow hunting."

"What about unicorn riding?" teased Lizzie.

Brendan was not amused. "Just watch for the stupid rainbow."

The drive continued on as the rain dissipated. The clouds were still hanging on strong, but the sun was able to peak through the cracks casting brilliant rays of light over the Irish landscape. Both kids were awestruck, but neither spoke about it. Brendan wondered if she felt the familiarity in what they were looking at as well.

Before too long, the storm began to die off. Brendan shut off his wipers as the last few drops of rain splashed on the windshield. "How much longer are we going to search, Liz? I mean we're down to…" He glanced down at his gas gauge and was pleasantly surprised. "Huh? It's still on full. These little foreign cars do get good gas mileage."

Lizzie searched the sky to no avail and allowed her shoulders to slump. She sighed. "I don't know. I guess we can turn around…if you want to…" She stopped in mid-sentence because something caught her eye. "Wait! I see one!"

The misty haze before them thinned slightly and Brendan also spotted the faded colors of a distant rainbow. The closer they got, the rainbow that had looked faded and so far away grew more brilliant. It beckoned them.

"Whoa!" exclaimed Brendan. "Look at the size of that thing!"

The rainbow shimmered in dazzling hues, radiating from a huge thundercloud that no longer dropped its heavy drops. Lizzie's mouth hung wide open at the sight of the thing.

"It's so beautiful," she whispered.

Brendan and Lizzie drove toward the rainbow and Brendan had to marvel at how the road to get there was so traversable. Unlike rainbows in America, or anywhere else for that matter, this rainbow stood still, transfixed, rooted in a single unmovable location. Brendan found road after road that wound the car on a fairly direct route to the prize. When he finally turned onto a gravel road that lead directly into a thick forest, Brendan brought the car to a stop.

"Corways," he read from an old wooden sign that guarded the dark entrance.

Brendan looked over at Lizzie to gauge her panic level about entering the dark forest and when she gave him a small nod, he slowly accelerated and their world was swept away with shadows. Only what lay in the path of the dim headlights was visible. Brendan was happy that the road was among the things that the light touched.

It was eerie. This much darkness wasn't normally found topside of the Earth. Caves can hide light pretty well during the day, but a forest typically allowed a modicum of light to peak through. Even the rainbow had been hidden by the thickness of the canopy. They hoped that they were still on the right track.

"It's kind of scary back here," said Lizzie with a nervous laugh.

"We should be coming up on Corways any moment," replied Brendan. He was trying to comfort both of them. He wouldn't admit it to her at the moment, though, since someone needed to be calm and in control. He just hoped she couldn't see well enough in the dark to notice his hands slightly trembling on the steering wheel.

The further on they drove, the thinner the forest became. It was subtle, but there was enough space in the trees for the rainbow to reappear. Occasionally, Brendan had to turn on his wipers to swipe away the drops of water that could no longer cling to the leaves and branches overhead.

The car wound around the trees and Brendan steered the little smoking car nimbly around the obstacles until he came to a dead end. A massive tree had toppled over at some point and laid crossways across the road.

"Looks like the end of the road," Brendan said wryly.

"But we're almost there," Lizzie chirped. "Look!"

Sure enough, through the tree line shone the brilliance of the rainbow in all of its glittery luster.

Brendan heaved out the breath a person does when he's about to do something that he doesn't want to do. He reached back behind the passenger seat and pulled out a small emergency kit. He unzipped it and examined the contents. There was a flashlight, band-aides, gauze, iodine, medical tape, and rubber gloves all packed inside the little drawstring bag. He removed the flashlight and then handed the bag over to Lizzie. He cut the engine and put the keys in his pocket as he exited his door. Lizzie popped out from the other side.

"If we're going to go on, then you carry the bag."

Lizzie shrugged. "Fine. Let's go."

They paused and examined the surroundings. There was only overgrowth and large trunks to see. Lizzie's face held a quizzical look.

"What's the matter?" asked Brendan.

"How could a place that I've never been feel so

familiar?"

"You feel it too?" Brendan said in surprise. "Crazy, huh?"

"I know, right?"

They smiled nervously, both confused over the weirdness of the idea.

"Well, if we're going to do this, then let's get to it," Brendan declared.

He led the way over the fallen tree with the flashlight in hand and Lizzie followed close on his heels. He shone the beam of light around and then turned to his sister.

"Now be careful, Liz. It's really dark and we don't know what this ground is like."

"I know, I know." She rolled her eyes. "The rainbow ends just past those trees. Come on, let's go."

Brendan looked out into the mist and darkness and found the dirt, gravel, and mulch-like path. He could see the rainbow beyond, looming gracefully in its shine, but there were too many trees in between them and their prize to get a full view.

He led Lizzie down the path as the route began to slope and narrow. It was so steep that they found their ankles were having to point their toes and their upper bodies were starting to lean backwards. Brendan tried to slow his pace but with Lizzie right on his tail, it was growing more and more difficult.

"Stop pushing me," snapped Brendan when the pace continued to quicken.

"Go faster!" Lizzie exclaimed, pushing her brother

harder. "What if the rainbow disappears, then we miss seeing...whatever!"

"Stop! We're going too fast!"

Lizzie must not have heard, or perhaps she didn't care, because her shoving and forward motion carried the siblings faster and faster down the slope. It was all Brendan could do to not go tumbling like Jack and Jill. Brendan tried to focus his light ahead, but it was bouncy and scattered. At the last moment he saw that they were coming to an abrupt drop off.

"Whoa!" he yelled as his foot planted on an embedded rock at the very edge of the path. He teetered on his balance point and had just enough of a view to look over the drop. His arms flailed and his core wavered as he stared into the darkness below. In this low light Brendan had no idea how far he would fall if he didn't steady himself. Luckily for him, he managed to hold his place.

Lizzie charged forward having seen her brother in trouble. "I've got you!"

Brendan didn't turn in fear of falling, but he called out for her to stop, but it was too late. Lizzie was running too hard and tripped in the darkness on a root or a rock, and she slammed into Brendan. The momentum sent them careening over the edge and into the dark.

Ten feet down they slammed into a natural drainage slope sopped with flowing muddy water. It twisted around tree trunks and eroded chucks of hill and ground hurtling them faster and faster until they were dropped fifty feet into a retaining pool.

Brendan felt the sting of the cold water on his skin as he pulled at the water to reach the surface. It was a bit of a struggle, but he managed to burst from the water and gulped a needed breath. Water ran through his eyes and made it hard to see.

"Lizzie!" he called. "Lizzie, where are you?"

His heart nearly stopped as his call went unanswered. They always gave each other a hard time, but he knew he was her protector. He would never let anything happen to her, but here they were in an Irish drink and he had lost her. He called out again and his heart was ready to jump from his chest.

Coughs and gasping came from somewhere to his left. "Lizzie!" His sister hacked and coughed up some of the water. "You okay? Swim to the edge."

He tore through the water toward her but she had already begun to make her way to the pool's shore line. He helped her get out and followed her onto the grassy bank. Now that she was okay, he stared at her with a look that could kill.

She finally noticed. "What?"

"I told you not to push me, didn't I?"

Lizzie couldn't believe her ears. "I was trying to save you. Remember, clumsy?"

"Save me?" Brendan laughed. "You were the one…"

"Shhh!"

Brendan looked at his sister in absolute shock. "Don't shhh, me. You about killed us!"

"Shhh! Stop being a baby," she said to his astonishment.

"Do you hear that?"

Brendan wasn't sure, but he thought he heard something. Perhaps it was music or some bird, but it didn't matter at the moment. His sister had just insulted him and he wasn't about to stand for it. Before he could reply, Lizzie was up and moving toward the direction of the noise.

"I'm not being a baby," he mumbled. "I just wanted to be careful on a dark, slippery hill. That's all."

Lizzie pulled back a large bough and a bright light shone through the space. She smirked at him. "I think I found something. Come on."

She vanished through the brush before he could reply. He had to hustle to keep up. "Wait up."

Brendan pushed limbs and bushes aside as he tried to follow his sister. She had a bit of an advantage on him being shorter and thinner. She probably slipped through the tight landscaping with little hindrance where he was getting swacked by branches and leaves every second or so. He emerged from the brush with a mouthful of greenery. He spat it out and spotted his sister standing near the rear of a beat-up old wooden cottage towards the edge of what appeared to be a town.

He scampered up to her. "Why didn't you wait on me?" He noticed that the sky was lit in the direction of town.

She glanced back at him and smirked. "Did you lose your flashlight and get scared?"

"I wasn't scared," Brendan said defensively. "Something could've happened to you, that's all."

The noise grew louder momentarily. "There it went again," Lizzie said with her ears perked. "Sounds like it's from the center of town."

"We'll check it out, but let's take it slowly this time. We don't know what we're going to find when we get there."

Lizzie shrugged. "Fine."

They crept away from their cover and walked to the next house. They looked around the wall and finally had a clear view of the light source. They had to partially shield their eyes from the rainbow, which had become blindingly white. Gradually the light separated into the spectrum of colors revealing the most glorious red, orange, yellow, green, blue, and violet that they had ever seen.

"It's so beautiful," marveled Lizzie.

Brendan couldn't deny the assertion. He had flown over Las Vegas last summer on his way to San Diego for the Soccer Nationals and at the time he thought that it was the most beautiful display of lights that he had seen. This made Vegas look like Christmas lights on an abandoned gas station.

They moved toward another home and stayed hidden from the center of town. When they looked out toward the rainbow this time they caught sight of dark movements where the rainbow was touching the ground. Brendan took another more studied look at the scene. The rainbow didn't actually touch the ground, but faded some ten feet above it. The colors didn't just stop, but rather dissolved into metallic sparks and sprayed the ground beneath it like confetti.

Lizzie pointed and covered her mouth. She was nearly jumping up and down.

"Shhh! Stop moving," said Brendan.

"Look! Leprechauns!" Lizzie whispered in a screechy way.

Brendan was still watching the rainbow's light show and hadn't really been observing the dark figures moving at ground level. "That's ridiculous! It's probably just your imagination." His eyes moved away from the sparks and the biggest rainbow ever to the shadows, but he never allowed his eyes to drop all the way to the ground since a much taller figure captured his attention.

"Dorian!" he said in disbelief.

Lizzie followed Brendan's stare. "Who? That girl?"

"I met her two nights ago," he replied.

"Oh, that's right. Your girlfriend from the parking lot."

Still defensive even in the midst of this tremendously unbelievable scene, Brendan retorted, "Shut up."

Lizzie snickered a little but dropped her eyes quickly to the shadowy figures moving about on the ground. She wanted to see them clearly, but they were just out of the light.

Brendan continued to watch Dorian. She was beautiful. Perhaps even more beautiful than the rainbow and its dazzling sparks. She must have been by the way he stared. She was smiling and laughing. Brendan didn't notice the burst of sparks that lit the ground exposing dozens and dozens of dancing little people. He didn't see that they had large cauldrons on wooden pushcarts collecting the spray and sparks of color. He didn't hear the small people playing instruments and singing in jubilance. All he saw was Dorian, and all he thought about was their first encounter.

"This is amazing!" laughed Lizzie. "What do you think they're doing?"

Brendan was still lost in Dorian.

"Brendan?"

"Huh?" Brendan pulled himself out of thought. "I don't know what they're doing, Liz."

He looked back at the Irish beauty just as a terrifying shriek filled the air. Dorian's smiled vanished as she searched the sky. The music and dancing stopped and the little people began the scatter. A second shriek resounded in the air and Brendan and Lizzie covered their ears along with all of the little people and Dorian.

"What was that?" asked Lizzie.

Brendan looked to the sky to find the answer. Through the bright rainbow a dark shadow soared. It flapped its expansive wings as it drew closer. The shadow shrieked again just as it burst through the rainbow shattering the light and sending colorful sparks in all directions. With the rainbow gone, the town fell into grayness. A depressing contrast to say the least. Brendan spotted the creature on its second dive toward the town. It was massive with a fifteen-foot wingspan and a body that was at least as long. It had the head of an eagle with a beak that could easily tear a cow in half. Its front claws had two-foot long talons that scraped and clanged off of the others. Its body was muscular and was frighteningly like a lion's all the way down to the golden pelt that covered it. Its back legs were even more lion-like. It was the most frightening thing either of the O'Neal kids had ever seen, or heard of, for that matter.

"I think that's our answer," he said, swallowing down the lump in his throat.

They hunkered down behind the building, but neither could stop watching the horrific scene. The creature hovered over the town by flapping its wings. It created such a vortex of wind that it reminded Brendan of the horrific tornado videos he had seen online. The beast swooped down and swiped a huge claw at a group of scampering little people. They ran, but the creature was faster. It's claw tore through a handful of the frightened people tearing them to bits and causing them to shatter into a burst of sparks. Six others barely evaded the beast's bloodthirsty attack.

The entire scene was so sickening and brutal. Brendan and Lizzie clung to each other and more than one silent prayer was uttered between the pair. These small people were being slaughtered. The creature dove over and over again leaving havoc in its wake. The people scampered to sometimes-useless hiding places only to be murdered in mid-scream. The beast rose again and this time its piercing eyes fixated on one target. It pulled at the air and shot like a bullet at this one little person. The man held his ground and raised his hands. They began to glow a bright orange but the creature was on him in the blink of an eye.

Brendan cringed expecting to see the little man blasted to dust, but the creature merely snatched him up and began to depart.

"Noooooooo!" screamed Dorian running to the spot where the little man had been. She dropped to the ground and reached into the air after the beast and his captive. Her eyes were leaking out tears and her face was that of sheer anguish. Silence was all around them.

Chapter 5
✝ The Quest ✝

THE CREATURE WAS LONG GONE before Lizzie could find her voice. "Oh my gosh."

The reaction was so slow only because the situation was so unbelievable. Should she scream? Should she run? Should she go have a psychological evaluation? Maybe, she thought.

The little people began to crowd around Dorian and lament their dead. Their faces and haunting songs told the story. They were terrified and confused and for some reason they were all looking to Dorian. Were they seeking comfort or direction? Lizzie was surprised that the young girl, even though Dorian was at least as old as Brendan, was what was holding these people together. She was even more surprised when Brendan stepped around her and walked over to where Dorian was and put his hand on her shoulder. The little people backed away quickly with cautious eyes on the stranger.

Lizzie jumped up and followed her big brother into the midst of the group. "Wait up." The little people backed away a few inches more and didn't appear to know how to handle the entire crazy situation.

"Dorian," Brendan said softly.

Dorian slowly lifted her face from the palms of her hands. Her eyes were red and her cheeks were flushed. "What are you doing here?" she asked in a voice that was just above a whisper.

"I…" Brendan struggled to complete the sentence. "I was going to ask you the same question."

Dorian's brow knitted closely together as she got to her feet. "I live here." She wiped the wetness from her cheeks and looked in the direction that the creature had flown.

"What just happened?"

Dorian swiped her nose on her sleeve and said, "A griffin has taken him. That's what happened."

"Who?" asked Lizzie.

Dorian walked down the center of town. "My father."

Lizzie and Brendan exchanged confused looks. Brendan jogged a few steps to catch up to Dorian. "Your father? How?"

Dorian strode ahead, clearly intent in her motion. "It's really none of your business, and this really isn't your concern."

They followed her to the threshold of a little house and she turned on them. "Go back home, Yank." She gave him a hard stare to make her point clear. "Forget everything you've just seen." She marched into an old cottage leaving the siblings in the street.

"Brendan, I don't know what it is, but I think we need to help her." Lizzie held Brendan's gaze with conviction.

"Liz…" he began, but he allowed his voice to drop off.

"Don't ask how I know that we need to help her, Brendan. I can't answer that question. Call it a feeling or destiny or whatever, but I know this is where we were meant to be and this is what we need to do."

He knew that she believed it. He knew that she meant what she said. He also knew what it meant to be her protector, and from the looks of things it didn't feel like this was going to be a pleasure walk. He turned from his sister and followed Dorian into the house.

"Maybe I can help," Brendan said hopefully.

Lizzie chimed in too. "Maybe we can help."

"You don't understand what we're dealing with here." She shook her head as if she was continuing to talk these two crazy Americans out of trying to help in a hopeless situation.

"But it's not dangerous for you? Come on, let me…"

Lizzie interrupted her brother. "…us."

Brendan withheld an argument to squash an outburst from Lizzie. "Let… us help you."

Dorian ignored him, or at the least pretended that he wasn't talking and marched past them to an old wooden cabinet. She opened the door with a loud, painful creak and began to root around. She pulled out herbs, a dusty book that probably hadn't been opened in three hundred years, a wooden soup ladle, and six vials of the brightest fluids that the O'Neal's had ever seen and laid the items on the table in the center of the room.

"Maybe they can help," came a voice that was very low to the ground and near the opening of the house.

Dorian never stopped studying the items when she replied, "What can they do, Biddy? They'd just get in the way or get themselves killed."

"Killed?" Brendan blurted out before he could stop himself.

"See what I mean?" Dorian gestured his way in frustration. "He lacks the courage."

Brendan wanted to argue, but maybe she was right. Maybe he wasn't the most courageous guy in the world, but he felt like he could help. He didn't always volunteer when he probably should have back in the States, but he knew Dorian needed him. He didn't know why, but Lizzie felt it too, so maybe that made it easier to offer.

The little woman that Dorian referred to as Biddy

screwed her eyes up in thought and considered Brendan for a moment. She looked at him longer and deeper than anyone else had ever stared at him before. It was unnerving and made him very uncomfortable.

"No," she said after what seemed like way too long of a time to stare at a person. "You're wrong about him. I can feel it."

Brendan stepped forward and put his hands on the table absently. "I'm willing to help, Dorian." He found that his index finger was trailing back and forth on the ancient book's spine.

"Me, too," Lizzie added enthusiastically.

Brendan turned to his sister. "If this is life or death, Liz, then I can't let you go." He continued quickly before she could argue. "I'd never forgive myself if something happened to you."

"I need to go." Her expression showed that she wasn't backing down.

A second small person entered the room. "Sorry, big fellow. The girl has to go."

"Wait. What?" Brendan said incredulously. "Who are you?"

Biddy, now sitting atop the table spoke up for the newcomer. "This is Rory. He has a gift for seeing the future."

Rory leapt from the floor to a chair to the spot next to his counterpart. "'Tis true, you know. Long ago I foresaw this day… or at least a shadow of this day."

Biddy, Brendan, and Lizzie stood and listened intently

as Rory told his tale. Dorian listened while she packed the tabled items into a backpack.

"Some three or four years ago a vision was given me," he began. "I saw the rainbow dissolve above our heads and a horrible shadow overtake the town. I knew that one of us would go missing. I felt a great sadness and loneliness."

"I bet he's the life of the party," whispered Lizzie.

"But, I also saw two shining figures of light and they appeared right after the shadow left us." Rory looked up hopefully at the siblings. "They joined three from our village and pursued the shadow."

Brendan thought aloud. "Well, we know what the shadow was and we know who went missing." He stole a glance at Dorian who kept her eyes on her backpack. The zippers and pockets must have been extremely interesting. "But, what I don't know is where the griffin took Dorian's father, or for that matter, why he was taken."

"The witch," Dorian said in a weak, frightened voice.

"Morna?" Biddy looked surprised to hear the accusation. "But she has always let us be. Why would she do this?"

"Don't you see, Bid? She wants my father's magic."

Brendan felt he had to interject at the mention of the "M" word. "Time out. Magic?"

Rory laughed. "You've just seen the end of a rainbow, a griffin, and a village full of Leprechauns, and you can't buy into magic?"

"He's always been a doubter," said Lizzie.

"I'm not doubting anything," said Brendan defensively.

"This is just a lot to take in." He turned toward Dorian. "Who is this Morna?"

"She's a very powerful witch."

"Why have we never heard of her before?" asked Lizzie. "You'd think someone with crazy power would be on the news a few times."

"Deary, she's not out there making herself known," said Biddy.

Rory nodded. "No, but I believe that Dorian's right. The witch is making a play at something."

It was Brendan's turn to laugh. "You don't know, Rory? You haven't foreseen it?"

Rory raised an eyebrow that spoke of his astonishment. "It's a gift. It's not like I'm running around getting visions all of the time, now am I?" He chuckled again. "That'd be plain silly."

"Right. So, what do we do?" Brendan asked Dorian.

Dorian zipped her last pocket shut and threw the bag on her back. "I'm going to the witch's castle. That's where she'll be holding him." She walked towards the door without indicating that she was taking anyone else along.

"Wait, Dorian." Rory jumped from the table and sprinted to block the doorway, well at least as best as he could. "You know I get these visions for a reason. We have to follow the instructions. Each of us in this room must go."

Dorian looked down at the little man and at each person in the room. "If that's the way it must be."

Rory held his arms up. "Before we go, I must give

warning. I know that sorrow is waiting upon us."

Lizzie gulped. "What do you mean?"

Rory nodded solemnly. "I'm afraid that we may each face our mortality and I fear that not all involved will survive."

"Gee, now I'm pumped about this," said Brendan sarcastically.

"Do you see?" huffed Dorian.

"Don't worry, Dorian. This one has great courage. It radiates from him," smiled Biddy.

Lizzie half-coughed and half-laughed. "How do you know that?"

Biddy shrugged. "Rory can see the future, I can tell a person's character."

Lizzie leaned in close to Biddy and in a hushed voice she asked, "What do you see in me?"

"I see a spirit full of love and intelligence," Biddy said truthfully.

Now it was Brendan's turn to half-cough and half-laugh. "You haven't seen her report card then."

"Shut up," protested Lizzie.

Dorian moved toward the door and spared a single glance back at the other four. "Come now. We're wasting time."

Brendan and Rory followed Dorian out the door and Lizzie and Biddy took the rear.

Lizzie smiled down at the tiny woman. "I knew I liked you, Biddy."

✦ ✦ ✦

Thunder clapped and lightning flashed all around a

big stone castle in the middle of a dark forest in Scotland. Creepy and sinister it sat, alone and sheltered from any passersby. The stories and myths that surrounded the Black Forest, as it became known, were the things of legend. Hellish tales of torture and nightmares, most of which weren't true, served to keep the old Scottish castle isolated and undisturbed. The mistress of the castle preferred it that way.

An unnatural silhouette soared among the storm clouds in a direct path to Morna's castle. Rain pelted the little man in the griffin's clutches. He shielded his eyes with his free hand since his other arm was bound tightly to his body in the strong grasp of the claw. Looking in the distance his eyes grew large as a flash of lightning backlit the ominous castle like a bad Frankenstein movie.

The griffin glided smoothly into the castle's tower and landed gracefully on the cold stone floor, dropping water on the floor and on top of the unwilling captive. Once the griffin had settled itself and the landing was complete, it tossed the little Leprechaun across the hard floor. The prisoner skidded and rolled until he landed at the feet of the mistress of the castle.

He looked up at the witch through foggy eyes and blinked out the moisture. "Morna?"

"Welcome to my humble home, Duncan." Morna turned away from the king of the Leprechauns and added, "I hope you had a pleasant flight."

She looked at a red-eyed slave who stood swaying in the corner and nodded slightly. He quickly walked over and snatched the diminutive monarch by the scruff of his coat.

Duncan struggled against the slave's hold to no avail. He looked over at Morna with questioning eyes.

"What do you hope to gain, witch?"

"Only your allegiance and all of you power," she laughed mirthlessly.

Duncan scoffed. "How do you intend to strip me of my power, Morna? The means no longer exists."

Morna smirked at the little man and exposed the hilt of a dagger to him. "Look familiar?" she said pulling the blade an inch or two from its sheath revealing the smooth black blade.

"That's not possible," whispered the king.

Morna hid the dagger once more and tilted her head at her guest. "Pity you don't have any of the rainbow's magic handy, eh?" Morna grinned cruelly. "I bet you could use a shot of that dust now."

Duncan didn't respond verbally. His hands glowed again and he sent a beam of orange energy at Morna. The witch casually deflected the magic and exhaled a black mist that enveloped the king. He fought against its effects, but his orange spark faded and then extinguished. He hung helplessly in the slave's thick hand as hope seemed to fade out of his mind.

Morna turned her gaze to the guard. "Show our guest to his new room."

The slave exited the tower at her command and left Morna alone with her griffin. She gently rubbed its beak as the storm raged on to her delight.

Chapter 6
✦ The Right Direction ✦

THE CLOUDS WERE FINALLY starting to retreat, giving Brendan a sense that the day was going to start looking up. Glancing at Dorian, he didn't get the impression that she was feeling the same way. He couldn't blame her, after all her father was just abducted by a mythical creature that shouldn't exist, so he kind of understood that she was in a weird place at the moment.

Lizzie took some time as they journeyed through town to check out all of the Leprechauns. They really didn't seem all that different from the people she had met in Galway, only they were miniature. It sort of went against everything she knew about Leprechauns, like what she had read or had seen in movies and on TV.

"I thought Leprechauns were all supposed to be little men with red beards and green clothes," she commented.

"You can blame Colym for that," Biddy replied rolling her eyes and pointing to a little red-bearded man in a green suit lounging on a rock, half-liquored up and stifling belches. "One night, after a long night of finding his way to the bottom of a few mugs, Colym let himself be seen. You can imagine how the stories grew from there."

Colym burped at that point, nearly vomiting up last night's meal, but only just managing to swallow it back down.

"Oh, I see." Lizzie nearly vomited herself, but she didn't want to hang out near the little disgusting man any longer than she had to.

Colym's head was a little roly-poly on his shoulders and he held it aloft like it weighed as much as the rock on which he sat. He held it steady just long enough to catch sight of Biddy and began to wave. His wave threw him off balance and he flipped head-over-heels backwards off his rock and out of sight.

"Oh, my gosh," shrieked Lizzie, holding her hand to her open mouth. "Is he okay?"

Biddy waved Colym's tumble off as no big deal. "He's fine. He does it all the time."

Lizzie shrugged and followed the group. When they reached the edge of the town she heard a loud, booming belch erupt from behind the rock. Birds scattered from the trees and Lizzie supposed that the little drunk was sleeping it off and was probably wetting his pants. She hustled to catch up after she heard another booming noise, only this time it didn't sound like it came from his mouth.

After a nice hike up a partially muddy, clod-stricken hill, Dorian and the others reached the large trunk that blocked the path where Brendan and Lizzie had abandoned their car. Dorian nimbly leapt over the trunk and strolled right past the O'Neal's junker.

"Whoa!" hollered Brendan as he hurdled the tree trunk. "Where are you going?"

Dorian paused and looked back, clearly frustrated. "I thought we already established that I was going to go and save my father."

"Yeah, I know, but why don't we just take my car?" said Brendan whose hand was on the door handle.

Rory stretched his back out and bent his knees up and down. "That sounds a whole lot better than walking."

Biddy nodded. "It is a long way to Morna's castle."

"Fine," conceded Dorian. "But I'm riding shotgun."

"Dang it," huffed Lizzie.

They started to load into the car and Biddy leaned over to Rory. "What's 'shotgun?'"

Rory just shrugged and leapt into the back seat.

✦ ✦ ✦

Somewhere on the journey from the tower to his holding cell, Duncan had lost consciousness. Had he been slammed into a wall or choked out or drugged? He wasn't sure but he knew that he had a headache that was threatening to split his skull apart. How long had he been in this cell? Minutes? Hours? Days? He couldn't tell.

Duncan began to regain his focus in spite of the headache and the darkness in the dungeon. His cell was more of a mobile cage with thick bars that were too close together for him to fit through. It had a solid wood base and top and was one of two cages in the room. Trapped like a bird in a cage, he noted.

When his eyes had adjusted as best as they could in the little light allowed, he examined the other cage. A small figure was laying in a heap groaning. The little body was rocking gently in the fetal position in apparent pain.

"Wardicon?" said Duncan softly. The Sidhe King did not reply. He continued to groan and rock, saddening Duncan further. "Morna has attacked the Sidhes as well, has she?"

Duncan walked to the bars nearest the Sidhe's cage and tested them. They were solid iron and unbreakable for a Leprechaun that currently was without magic. Wardicon sat up with his back to Duncan and sharply adjusted his neck. His body rose in an unnatural movement like a puppet on invisible strings.

"Wardicon, what has she done to you?" Duncan called

to the fairy.

Wardicon shifted his body in an eerie fashion and shot Duncan a fierce look with a snap-turn of his head. The Sidhe King's features were his own, only depraved. His eyes were sunken deep within their sockets and his skin had lost its normal hue having faded to a light gray. Wardicon's hair was matted and greasy falling in strings across the once proud king's face. His wings were unfurled and were revealed to be more bat-like now as opposed to their original sheer appearance. Wardicon ran toward the bars attempting to attack Duncan, but he found that the bars were unwavering on his end as well. The Sidhe shook the cage with unexpected strength as he clawed and hissed at the distraction in the room. After finding no way to get to Duncan, Wardicon slunk back down to the floor and into his fetal position, soothing himself once more on the oak base of his cage.

Duncan was shocked and confused. He had never seen anything like that. That dagger was apparently all that the legends claimed it to be and now it was in Morna's possession. He had to wonder if he and Wardicon were going to share the same fate.

✦ ✦ ✦

Oscar entered the records' room with high hopes. All of his research had led him back to this point and this small, dank room in the corner of the public library. The building was small and had a tiny general store on the back side of it. The two were separated by a wall, but the hum of the refrigerators could be heard coming through the wall.

He expected to have to work really hard to find what he was looking for, but it just so happened that when he walked into the room, there were three leather-bound books sitting on the table. He sat his stuff down and just picked one up intent on putting it back on the shelf, but the wording on the spine caught his attention.

"O'Neal," he read aloud. "What luck!"

He proceeded to open the book, and low and behold there were several pages marked. He flipped to the first and began to read about the clans that lived in the area. There were tons of family names that were common in both Ireland and America. He smiled like a schoolgirl and moved on the next bookmark and the next and the next. He furiously took notes and then cross referenced the information with the other two books that were sitting on the table.

"I wonder why these books were just laying out?" He knew it was probably too good to be true, but he needed a break in this research. He had been working for years to pinpoint the family roots, and here was some of the information that he needed.

All he had to do now was go to Gilshery and continue the work. Perhaps finally there was a little of that Irish luck that he had heard so much about on his side.

Oscar stepped back into the main room of the library and shuffled over to the counter.

"Excuse me, but how would one go about getting to Gilshery?"

The clerk looked up half asleep and half confused. He shrugged and then took a large swig of cold coffee. Most of the gelatinous liquid made it into the guy's mouth. Most of it.

"I'm heading to Gilshery," called a voice from the doorway.

Oscar turned and saw a well-dressed gentleman smiling with an extended hand. He was extremely pale, but had the darkest hair he had ever seen.

"The name's Charlie," said the stranger.

Oscar took his hand and shook. "I'm Oscar."

"Look, you're welcome to come along with me to Gilshery. I was just about to leave now."

Oscar cringed. "Oh, well, I needed to drop by my hotel and leave some money for my kids, first, but I don't want to hold you up."

"Nonsense," replied Charlie. "It will only take a tic, and besides, this town isn't all that big."

"Well, I appreciate the ride, friend. I'll call them on the way."

Oscar followed the man to the expensive Mercedes and slid into the front seat.

Driving out of Corways, Brendan found that the conversation quickly gave way to silence. The hum of the 2.5 liter engine and the movement of wind were the only sounds around. Lizzie and Biddy had settled for staring out of the side windows from the back seat. Dorian stared ahead, sullen and contemplative, and Rory perched on

Brendan's seat back.

"Brendan, have you been holding out magic on us?" commented Rory after a time.

"Huh?"

"You've got your pocket flashing with some fancy colors," Rory pointed out.

Brendan glanced down at his pocket and noticed the red and blue lights of his smart phone showing through his apparently too thin khaki pants. He would have to remember to not wear that pair to school. It would make it a lot harder to get away with texting if the teachers could spot when he had a text or a call before he could.

"Oh, that's my phone." He pulled it out and saw his dad's name on the LCD display as a missed call. "It was Dad, Liz."

Brendan slid the bar and then pressed the screen and held the phone out. Oscar's message played over the speakerphone. "Brendan, I hope you and Liz are having a great time here in Galway. Listen, kiddo, I need to get over to a little town called Gilshery. I have a lead that I need to follow. I'll be back in a couple of days. I left you some money in the room. Love you guys. Call me anytime. I'll be checking in with you every now and again. Enjoy the car; I caught a ride. See you later."

"Gilshery?" Rory asked with a twisted-up expression. "Why on Earth would someone want to go to Gilshery?"

Brendan shrugged. "It's our dad; he's looking up family history."

"We have ancestors that went to the U.S. from here,"

added Lizzie.

Biddy leaned forward. "What's the name that he's looking for?"

"O'Neal," answered Lizzie.

Rory perked up at the name. "You don't say. We used to have plenty of O'Neals back in Corways."

"That's what some drunk told us, too." Brendan rolled his eyes thinking back to the experience in the pub. It seemed like a year ago, but it had only been about a day since they had heard that crazy tale from that pub full of nut jobs.

A thought, a terrible and slightly disgusting thought entered Brendan's mind and he looked over at Dorian. "Uh, your last name isn't O'Neal, is it?"

Dorian came out of her thoughts. "Me? No, I'm a MacFlannery."

Brendan breathed a sigh of relief. "Good," he said looking away.

"Okay, I have to ask," said Lizzie sitting on the edge of the tiny back seat. "Does anyone know where we are going?"

Dorian opened her bag and pulled out a fairly large feather. It was golden and shimmered in the spotty sunlight. She set it on the seat between herself and Brendan and the feather righted itself like a compass.

"Whoa!" exclaimed Lizzie. "What kind of feather is that?"

"It's one of the griffin's feathers," explained Dorian. "It must have fallen off when it took my father."

"A griffin is not supposed to lose its feathers," added Rory. "It can't grow any new ones, so each feather is very important to it."

"So, what, the feather is trying to get back to the griffin then?" Lizzie asked a bit confused.

"Pretty much," answered Biddy.

Brendan raised a brow. "Well, then I guess we have our heading. Does anyone know where that is?"

Dorian nodded. "To Morna's castle. The griffin lives there, so if we follow the feather's directions, then that should lead us to my father."

"All right, but I want to stop off at our room and get some things and the money," Brendan said as Galway came into view.

Brendan and Lizzie left the car running on the curb as they took the steps two at a time to reach the entrance on the front porch of Gordy's Home. Mr. and Mrs. Gordy were planted in their normal chairs doing their favorite activity. Gordy paused mid-rock when the O'Neal kids reached the porch.

"Hey, Yank," Gordy began. "Your father wants you to call him on his cell phone when you get in."

"Oh, okay," Brendan replied as he grabbed the handle of the screen door.

"Be a good boy and call your father," echoed Mrs. Gordy.

"I will, ma'am," Brendan reassured her.

When they reached their suite, they grabbed a gym bag that Brendan had stuffed all of his toiletries into. He dumped it out and then grabbed the deodorant and put it back into the bag. He picked up snacks, the money, and some mints for fresh breath, just in case. Lizzie returned with soap, a towel, and shampoo.

"Soap and shampoo?" Brendan wondered aloud. "You think we're heading where there's a Ritz on every corner?"

Lizzie stuffed the products into the bag. "All I know is that I'm going to be in a car for a couple of days with you people, so I am not going to let any of you smell the car up." She wagged her finger and shook her head for emphasis. "We are bathing."

"Now that you mention it, Rory was a little rancid."

Lizzie nodded her head. "Imagine how he'll smell in two days."

Brendan considered it for a moment. "Maybe you should grab another bar or two."

Five minutes later they emerged onto the porch and began walking past Mr. and Mrs. Gordy.

"Off again so soon?" inquired Mrs. Gordy.

Gordy leaned forward and spoke in a loud whisper. "Didn't you see that nut job he's got in the car? Dorian, I believe."

Mrs. Gordy studied the passenger without trying to hide her stare. "So he does. Bad news, she is."

Gordy looked back to Brendan. "Bit of advice, lad, lose the harpy as soon as you can. She'll bring nothing but trouble."

Brendan and Lizzie exchanged glances. He was annoyed at the old couple for insulting Dorian and he wanted to give them a piece of his mind, but he only said, "Okay." Better to not talk to them any more than he had to.

They skipped down the steps and heard another reminder to call their father. Getting into the car, Brendan tossed the gym bag onto the back seat. He put the car into gear and tried to forget about Gordy's warning.

"You probably should call Dad," said Lizzie while Biddy took a new position on top of the gym bag.

"I will."

Rory's nose began to twitch and then he began to sniff the air like a hound tracking a rabbit. "Why do I smell soap?" he asked suspiciously.

Brendan and Lizzie smiled at each other. Who knew when they would have a chance to smile again.

Chapter 7
✛ Flight of the Sidhes ✛

THE EVER-STORMY AREA around Morna's castle rattled the air and energized the electrons causing strike after strike. The moat at the castle's base was alive with slithery creatures craving an unsuspecting caller or perhaps a girl scout with a wagon full of cookies.

Morna was nearly giddy at the thought of the plan. They

were nearly complete and soon the rule of man would be over and the wizards and witches that once dominated Europe would reign supreme once again. None of the others even knew of her plan, except for Conchar, of course, but he had long since went into hiding, leaving her alone and brewing. It surprised her that her mentor had not wanted to follow through on his own design, but he had planted the idea in her that it could work, and that was good enough for her. The old wizard probably didn't have it in him so he left it to the next generation. Fine by her.

She considered these things as she marched briskly down the stone hallway toward the dungeon. She pointed her finger at the door and threw her arm to the side and invisibly forced the door open, slamming it into the wall. She strutted inside and grinned at Duncan.

Duncan jumped to his feet and yelled, "What did you do to Wardicon?"

Morna cackled the evil laugh that haunts dreams and scares children. "Do you like his new look?" She spared a glance his way. "I hear everyone in our hidden world is wearing it these days. Or at least they will be."

Duncan folded his arms in defiance. "What are you talking about?"

"Poor little Wardicon and his Sidhes are only one step, Duncan," Mornan began.

"The Sidhes are a peaceful clan, but look at what you've made of their king!"

Morna tipped her head to the side in a consenting nod.

She walked over and touched the top of Wardicon's cage causing blue electricity to travel throughout. Wardicon leapt to the air in anger, flapping his bat-like wings and shrieking in a high-pitched, unrecognizable cry. He clawed at the witch before collapsing to the base unconscious.

"Such dark beauty I've created, isn't it?" She removed her hand and licked her lips in enjoyment as his little body continued to convulse. "And to think, Wardicon was nothing more than what you say. Peaceful. Dull. Not under my control."

"But why?" implored Duncan. "You've kept to yourself for all these years, why attack the Sidhes?"

"What do you think I've been doing for the last hundred and fifty years, Duncan? Getting my nails done?" She scoffed and then looked down at her fingernails, noticing that perhaps she was due for a manicure. "I've been reading and training for, I don't know, taking over the world. You know, forming it into my idea of a utopia."

"Apparently you mean pain and misery for everyone."

"Now you're catching on," she cheered. "The humans and the clans who agreed to this self-imposed hiatus will especially suffer."

"But why hold him here like that?" Duncan gestured at the sad mass that lay in a convulsing heap. Wardicon's wing was crumpled awkwardly beneath his frame.

"To make it simple enough for your little mind to comprehend, Duncan, I just need to possess the keeper of a clan's magic and cast a few spells from magic long forgotten to be in control of the clan."

"So, as long as you have him, you control the Sidhes?" Duncan shook his head in disbelief. "But why would you need to?"

Morna raised her brow. "You'd be surprised at how powerful the Sidhes are, Leprechaun. As a matter of fact, a little demonstration may be in order."

"What are you talking about?"

"When you arrived I noticed that my griffin was missing a feather. He wants it back."

Duncan was still confused. "I don't have its feather."

"I know that, simpleton. It seems to be traveling towards us as we speak, but the search party from your village is taking their sweet time about it. I think I'll send the Sidhes to get it back for my pet." She stared at Duncan waiting for his response.

"None from my village had better be harmed, Morna!" Duncan was reaching through the bars grasping at his much larger foe. "I'm warning you!"

Morna walked to the door deliriously happy with herself. "I heard that your daughter is leading the expedition, Duncan."

"Dorian," whispered Duncan.

"Dorian, you say? Don't worry, Papa Elf, I'll make sure the head stone is engraved appropriately." She exited the room in a fit of laughter leaving the Leprechaun King in helplessness and despair.

✦ ✦ ✦

The day was drawing closer to an end though the sun

had not totally retreated. Light was low but Brendan was able to appreciate the scenery once again. How beautiful was this country? It was green and open, and it was starting to make Brendan sleepy, and that was not a good thing for a driver. It didn't help much that everyone else in the car was quiet or dozing. The sounds of sleep were a nice incentive to drift off. He found himself shaking his head and wiping his eyes quite a bit as his little beat-up car bounced down the road.

"Are you awake?" Dorian asked. She happened to glance over and recognize the signs of fatigue.

Brendan smiled sleepily at the lovely creature in the passenger seat. The light was such that it really showcased her ridiculous beauty.

He waved her off. "I'm a little tired, but I'll be fine."

"I can drive if you want me too," she offered.

His tired mind thought back to the sheer craziness of her one time behind the wheel. He shot back to lucidness and said, "No, no. I'm up and very alert… now." He cleared his throat. "Is the feather still pointing us in the right direction?"

Dorian smiled knowingly and looked down at the griffin's feather. "It is."

Brendan, thinking he dodged an argument, looked ahead and spotted a dark blob in the air on the horizon. "What is that?"

Dorian caught herself staring at the handsome American. "What?" She knew Brendan did have something going for him, but she couldn't decide what it was.

Brendan pointed in the direction of the dark blob, which happened to be getting larger. "Up there."

Dorian squinted and then the realization floated into her mind. "No, it couldn't be."

"What? What is it?"

"They don't come down this far." Dorian's mind was confused. "They stay to themselves."

"Who does?" implored Brendan. He was getting annoyed at the lack in exchange of information.

"It's the Sidhes."

The large flock of Sidhes approached at an accelerated rate. A roiling mass of bat-like creatures with bared fangs and antsy claws poised to tear and slash. The one-time humanoid beings that were more along the lines of fairies that little girls had tacked up on posters in their rooms now held no such comparison. Gaunt and gray, the Sidhe nation had mutated into the things of nightmares. The only difference was that they were in the real world flying over an Irish road, intent on murder.

"What's a Sidhe?" asked Brendan.

"Uh, I believe you call them fairies."

"Oh, okay." Brendan considered it a moment. "Fairies are harmless, right?"

Suddenly, one of the deranged beings slammed into the windshield with a grimace-causing Smack!

"Whoa!" yelped Brendan, studying the hideous thing that had its sharp and not very sanitary looking claws digging into the glass. It took to opening its mouth and slobbering all over Brendan's line of sight. "Fairies? Fairies my foot!"

Three more Sidhes followed suit and slammed into the little car's windshield. The impacts left cracks, but the glass held. The ugly little things clawed and pulled and bit. A chubby one took a moment to gnaw on a big moth that hit the windshield ten or so miles earlier.

"They're Sidhes, but they've been changed somehow," Dorian replied.

Brendan had mashed on the gas trying his best to lose the weird things. More of the bat-wannabes slammed into the car. Some hit the hood and others the doors and roof.

Lizzie sat bolt upright, clearly still half asleep. "What's going on?" she asked sleepily.

Brendan flicked on his windshield wipers and surprised a few of the Sidhes. The rubber and metal smacked them in the face and sent them flying up and over the car. One clung to the wiper and bit large chunks out of it.

"Nothing," lied Brendan. "Go back to sleep, Liz."

"Okay," nodded Lizzie. She yawned and leaned her head against the side window. She settled in and was drifting back to sleep when an ugly mutant fairy smashed into the glass right next to her face. Lizzie opened her eyes and slowly recognized that she was awake. After getting a full look at the little monster, she shrieked loud and long. The Sidhe outside her window covered its ears and lost its grip. The wind and another Sidhe banged into it and sent it to the roadside.

Biddy and Rory, now awake with instant headaches

from the head-splitting scream, took in the battle scene.

"Are those Sidhes?" asked Biddy.

"I think so," answered Rory.

"What the do they want?" Brendan jerked the wheel and worked to knock off more of the things, but there were so many it became difficult to see through the thick mass of the ugly gray mutants.

Brendan's question lead Dorian to a realization. She looked down at the feather on the bench seat. "They're after the feather! They're working for Morna!"

Rory and Biddy exchanged looks of shock and sadness. What did that mean? Had the world they had always known vanished somewhere along the way? How could they have missed the signs?

"What do we do?" Lizzie yelled.

Brendan narrowed his eyes. "We get rid of them."

"How?" chortled Rory at the absurdness of the entire situation. "You don't know the Sidhes like we do. You don't just get rid of them."

Brendan moved his head, jockeying for a clear patch of vision and when he found it he smiled. He locked eyes on a group of large trees with low-hanging, heavy branches and he steered right at them. He didn't slow or hesitate. He didn't ask for permission or wait for the suggestion. He slammed the gas pedal down and rocketed the car off the road and into the growth.

The others screamed, but no one protested. They watched as the branches battered the gray Sidhes. The little things were knocked silly and sent flying. The branches also crashed into the windshield and spider webbed the entire thing. When they emerged out of the growth of trees, the car was mutant-fairy free.

"Boo ya!" cheered Lizzie.

More congratulations resounded from the others, but Dorian was watching the skies.

"We're not out of the woods yet," she warned.

"Yes, we are." Biddy pointed back to the trees. "Didn't you see us leave them?"

A collective scream materialized from the darkening sky. Two more caterwauls sounded and then the roof was assaulted. The most horrific scraping sounds and clawing came from above their heads. The even more frightening part happened next. The Sidhes' claws found thin spots in the rusting roof and they began to peel it away like a banana skin.

The car was alive with batting hands and screams. One Sidhe slipped in during the chaos and nicked the feather. It instantly took to the air and avoided Dorian's grasp.

"They've got the feather!" she shouted.

Brendan scanned the sky and spotted the little thief trying to hide amongst the others who had apparently regrouped for another offensive. "I see it."

"I can't let them get away with it," whispered Dorian.

She unzipped her bag and thrust her hand inside. She plucked out a vile with a golden liquid sloshing around and glowing. She poured the vile into her hands and the golden liquid absorbed into her palms. Her hands began to glow and radiated an energy that Brendan and Lizzie had never known before. Dorian took a deep breath and looked over at Brendan. Her eyes were no longer green and surrounded by white sclera. Instead her eyes blazed with golden magic.

The howl of war sounded above and Dorian exhaled. She thrust her hands through the opening in the roof as the glow intensified. She concentrated and emitted a blast of golden energy from the palms of her hand into the flock of Sidhes.

Brendan's jaw was wide open watching the golden streak of magic cut through the air and obliterate five Sidhes as if they were just guinea pigs in a nuclear bug zapper.

"Whoa! You got 'em!" shouted Lizzie.

"I was aiming at the thief," said Dorian.

Several other Sidhes began their attack again and dove right at their car.

"Forget the feather. Worry about the others!" snapped Brendan.

Dorian sited the dive-bombers and disintegrated them easily, but in the melee, the feather thief had flown away. The other mutant fairies flanked the thief and the battle was over.

"It's gone," lamented Dorian, her golden glow fading as quickly as it had come. Brendan brought the car to a halt, and Dorian leaned back in her seat. "How are we going to find him now?"

Biddy and Rory leapt to her shoulders and tried to comfort her.

Rory pursed his lips. "Don't lose heart, Dorian. The Sidhes gave us a direction to start with at least."

"We'll find him," promised Biddy.

Brendan pushed the gas pedal and somehow found a road going in the same direction as the Sidhes were flying. The car grew silent as the sun abandoned them.

✦ ✦ ✦

Morna spied the flock of Sidhes as they drew closer to her castle. She noted that their numbers were thin and their faces, though distorted to her liking, appeared frightened and shell-shocked.

The feather thief landed on the balcony first, followed closely behind by the fifty or so survivors. It stumbled forward, cradling the feather in its boney hands, and on trembling legs handed the prize over to the witch.

Morna, pleased with the mayhem her little slaves no doubt inflicted, took the feather and held it aloft. She had always enjoyed the dark, rich shadows the moon cast within the tower. The griffin stepped out of the shadows with its eyes as burning slits. Many of the Sidhes took to the air to avoid being in the same area as the fearsome predator. Morna turned the feather over in her fingers. When she did release it, the feather angled directly for its place on the griffin's right wing just behind the shoulder.

Morna turned her attention back to the group of Sidhe's on her ledge. "And what of the search party?"

She knew by the behavior that the little fools had failed in killing them. She knew that they had betrayed her in their failure. She lashed out and swatted the unfortunate few that were within arm's reach, scattering the remaining Sidhe's to the air.

Morna howled in anger and spun on her heels to rest against the stone rails of the balcony. "It appears that Duncan's daughter is more formidable than I thought. I'll need to send in Dullahan."

At the mention of his name, lightning struck the air and lit up the sky around the castle, thunder rolled, crying out in fear, and the mighty griffin slinked back into the shadows. Morna looked into the distance and could hear the approaching hooves of her champion's horse. Dullahan was on his way.

Chapter 8
✛ Visions ✛

IT WAS IN THE WIDE-OPEN PLAINS of Ireland that Brendan found himself enjoying a nice breeze and the smell of a stew boiling over the fire. He realized that his eyes were closed and he slowly opened them, but the sun was bright and unbearable and forced them to shut tight. He could feel them beginning to water in response.

He used his sleeve to push the tears away. He turned the opposite direction and blinked his lids open.

Once the stinging subsided, he looked around. He noted that he had never seen this place before, but somehow it was familiar. It was natural for him to be here. He didn't know why, but he could sense it.

There were aspens, sessile oaks, silver birch, and black alders among other groves of trees; nothing uncommon for the area. A small stream trickled by some thirty feet to the south and a family of fallow deer was bathing. Being from New York City, the closest he had been to nature was Central Park. The deer were amazing and they absolutely ignored him. He slowly walked towards them and they never budged. He managed to step within mere feet of them before they finally looked up in alarm.

"Whoa, I won't hurt you," he soothed. The deer must not have believed him because they sprinted away leaving no trace.

Brendan wiped his eyes again and then knelt down to the stream. He cupped his hands and tried to draw up water to splash his face. He tried, but found that he couldn't touch the water. His hands passed right through the stream without actually making any contact! They weren't even damp.

"Whoa!" he said aloud.

Small voices called out from the direction he had just come and he looked up expecting to see Biddy and Rory. Two little people waved and beckoned him to their campsite. He remembered the stew and began to follow the call. He kept thinking about the strangeness of the situation. When did Biddy and Rory start making stew? Where were Dorian and Lizzie? He didn't remember parking the car here. Hey, where was the car?

The closer he got to the small campsite the clearer it became that he didn't know these Leprechauns. They were both men with scraggly beards and shabby clothing. Now, Leprechauns normally dressed weird, but these two didn't wear anything close to what today's styles were. Brendan just assumed that they were backwoods Leprechauns, so he let the observation go unsaid.

"Hello," he greeted the men. They nodded. "Have you seen an ugly, rusted out, piece-of-junk car anywhere around here?"

Neither of the men replied. One stirred the pot while the other lit his long wooden pipe. As he stood there, waiting on the rude little men to respond, a third little man emerged from between his feet and joined the others at the fireside.

"Hello," Brendan repeated. "I'm talking to you."

They ignored him again. Instead, they addressed the newcomer.

"Evening, Cletus."

"How to do, Clive?" replied Cletus. "And you, Sean?" The little guy pulled up a stone and made himself comfortable.

Sean was stirring the stew and shrugged in response before he pulled the spoon out to test it. He smacked his lips and pulled out a couple of bowls. "Want some stew,

Cletus?"

"I don't mind if I do."

The bowls were filled and the three sat in silence slurping soup and annoying Brendan. It was obvious to him now that the little guys couldn't see him or just didn't want to see him.

"What word hear ye?" asked Sean.

Cletus wiped his mouth and frowned. "It ain't looking good, boys. I've got to be blunt," he paused, seeming to choose his words carefully before continuing. "I think that we may be headed for war."

"No!" gasped Clive.

"But I thought the Council was formed to prevent such a thing," added Sean.

"It was, but the wizards and witches will hear none of it," Cletus said. "They don't like the terms from what I hear."

"What terms would that be?" Sean shoved another heaping spoonful of mushroom stew into his gaping maw.

"The one about leaving the humans be. Conchar is a bad wizard with vengeance in his heart, I say."

Brendan listened to the conversation with peaked attention, but for some reason the words became hard to hear. He stuck his fingers in his ears to clear out the wax, but soon enough his lack of hearing turned into a lack of vision as well. The forest faded and everything went black. It was some time before his senses returned to him.

Shaking his head clear, Brendan found that he was on the ground with his back to a thick, bumpy trunk. His senses were sharp in contrast to the strange anesthetized mode he was trapped in moments before. He looked around and noticed that the winter snow was beginning to fall and the ground was just beginning to look frosted. Large flakes were gently floating down and Brendan looked up at them. The branches were bare and he had a pretty nice view of the cloudy sky. At that point, he wasn't sure where he was in the world, at least not judging by the surroundings, but his gut told him that he was still in Ireland. Maybe it was his gut, or just some innate sense of knowing, or maybe it was the two fairies that were perched on a low hanging bough.

"These winter days are so lovely," said the petite female Sidhe.

"Aye," agreed the older male with a short cropped beard. "Tis the last we'll see that will begin with peace, for some time, that is."

"Are things that bad?"

"They are, Orilla."

"Why can't the spellbinders just leave well enough alone, Bartamus?" she pleaded.

Bartamus shook his head sadly. "I think the spellbinders, like Conchar, hate the idea of not being the dominant ones. The humans are a different breed to be sure, but to try and wipe them out..." the Sidhe shuttered at the thought. "It's not right."

"Why isn't it?" Orilla frowned and stared into the distance, seemingly ashamed of the suggestion. "Isn't it better to have the wizards and witches killing them instead of killing us?"

Bartamus put his hand on the younger Sidhe's shoulder. "Easier, perhaps for a time. The question would be: Why would they stop there?" Orilla turned back to face the older fairy. "The humans are going to have their time in dominion, as our kind has, and it isn't for us to allow another to suffer. No, we will defend them because we can and we, the Sidhe, are a proud race that always tries to do what's right. Do you understand?"

Brendan observed the female's features and knew right off that she was very frightened. He also noticed how beautiful she was, nothing like the hideous flying uglies that attacked them earlier. Thoughts of Nerverland did enter his mind.

"I do understand," Orilla acknowledged. "But, Bartamus, the humans are cruel and vile creatures. They don't care for the Earth or its animals and plants! They don't even care for each other!"

"We magicks weren't any different, Orilla. We had our time to learn and to develop our race. They need that chance as well."

"Which side will the Merrows be on, Bartamus? And the Leprechauns?" The young Sidhe looked despairingly at her elder and waited.

"The Leprechauns are our cousins and they will side with us, but the Merrows are too self absorbed to recognize that their time is done. They will side with the spellbinders."

"And the spirits?" asked Orilla.

"I fear that the spirits will follow the wind," conceded Bartamus. "Their connections to this world depends on emotional beings, so their stake in this is only threatened if we all are destroyed."

Brendan looked up at the pair as they fluttered off into the air still conversing about the coming war. What did this all mean? Was he dreaming or was this something more? He didn't have too much time to ponder the thought since the snow began to fall as if an avalanche had just erupted. He tried to move, but he became buried and could no longer move. He grew so cold that time itself slowed and the light faded out.

The darkness was so cold. His breath was shallow and the freezing air burned his lungs. Was he really breathing? Is that what he felt, or was it something else? Spotty lights started to twinkle around him, but his vision was blurry and the lights were gingerly encompassed by halos. It was like looking through a pain of glass at the streetlights in the middle of a thunderstorm.

Little by little Brendan began to force his eyes into focus. It was hard to do and it took an enormous amount of will power, but he somehow managed it. It was still dark and though he knew his vision had returned, what he saw didn't make sense. The world was wavy and distorted. The sun's light was sparse and seemed far away. Shadows moved about him in unnatural ways.

"What is going on?" he yelled, only he could barely make out his own voice. It was like screaming in the pool.

One large shadow was sliding in his direction and the

realization of his location sent an elephantine amount of fear and adrenaline coursing through his veins. The shadow moved fast and smoothly and had a long tail complete with fins. Brendan pulled at the water around him, but managed to go nowhere. The creature moved closer and closer and Brendan turned his back and closed his eyes, bracing for the impact. When the figure moved past him he let out a breath.

At that moment a new panic hit him. He clutched at the water and slowly worked his way towards the surface. He had to get oxygen. He had to get oxygen fast … only he didn't have to get oxygen. He relaxed and realized that he didn't need it currently.

"Huh?" he said to himself. "No gillyweed for me, Mr. Longbottom. This guy can breath underwater!"

He spun and tugged on the water and found that when his mind was put to it, he could not only breath like a fish underwater, he could swim like one too! Another shadow appeared in the distance and then another. Soon he was in the midst of a swarm of large, blurry, black figures. They all swam with purpose in a single direction and Brendan felt the need to follow.

When the swim had ended, Brendan found himself floating amongst the shadows before a beautiful mermaid. All the shadows gave her their full attention and he decided to do so as well.

"As you all know, a war is coming that will threaten the Merrow way of life," the Queen Merrow began. "A new menace from the land has risen to prominence and they have their hearts set on conquering our seas, on ruining our traditions, and on plundering our inheritance."

Brendan could feel the anger brewing in the shadows. There was no noise of movement, but the water around him was growing warm, fueled by purpose and self-preservation.

"There are magicks who are to side with these heathens from the dry. Our kin who will work against us under false pretenses chortling with the enemy contriving for our end, our destruction, our extinction."

Brendan looked on the beautiful queen whose eyes were gray. He considered the contrast between her anger and her appearance. The heat around him grew until it became unbearable and he closed his eyes. The next thing he heard was the water around him coming to a boil.

The heat was intense and he had a sudden need to breath. He pulled down hard and made a path for the surface. He found it much faster than he imagined and sprang forth from the heated fluid to a hard surface. It took him a second to clear his eyes, but once he caught sight of where he was he wanted to close them again. The world was fuzzy once more and made him feel like he was hallucinating. He told himself that he probably already was.

Bang! Bang! Someone was hammering hard on wood. That was off in the distance, though, and too far for him to see. The sound was deafening anyway and he covered his ears with his hands. He chanced a look and stared up at another strange being and sighed. "Should I be surprised?" he mused aloud at the sight of a full-on, transparent, haunted house-looking ghost.

The ghost peered down at him. Brendan was taken aback. No one else had been able to see him. The ghost held one of its fingers to its see-through lips. Brendan took the hint and turned to spot another ghost across the room with a gavel levitating in its ghoulish grasp. The world apparently was now visible again so Brendan just rolled with it. His senses had been turned on and off so much he was left with no other option but to just go with it.

"Please be reasonable, Conchar," pleaded the ghost.

"There is no reason in the situation, Kleig!" argued a man in dark clothing.

That guy, Brendan thought was a bad individual to be around. Conchar oozed darkness. He wore dark clothes, had dark hair and fingernails. Even the whites of his eyes were darker than normal humans. Only his skin was white and it was such an unnatural white that Brendan guessed the man had been a shut-in for the last three-hundred years.

"Magicks are not going to be pushed around by mankind!" Conchar continued. "The very thought defies reason!"

"We have had our time," argued a Leprechaun. "Why can't you just go and exist in peace?"

"Perhaps you are ready to roll over and die but the necromancers will not!" Conchar's voice was raised and his tone dripped with venom. "Humans are not the next dominant species, my fellow magicks. No, I can promise you that their time will never come." The dark wizard looked around at the others gathered and so did the diminutive Brendan. He spotted a Leprechaun, a Merrow, a Sidhe, the two ghosts, and this one angery sorcerer.

"Are you threatening a war against the humans?" the Sidhe asked aghast. "The suggestion goes against our way."

"It goes against your way, perhaps, but not mine." Conchar narrowed his gaze before he spoke again. "Hear this now, the humans will not be allowed to be the ruination of this Earth, this land, or the spellbinders. You and your clans are either with me or against me. And know that when you are my enemy my mind drifts to murder."

To the Leprechaun's credit he stood up and defended his stance. "Then you have made an enemy of one of your closest friends, Conchar. The Leprechauns will stand between you and the humans."

"As will the Sidhes," spoke the small fairy.

Conchar sneered and looked over to the Merrow for her decision.

"Humans will ruin this world and my seas. We stand with the spellbinders," declared the Merrow.

Kleig slammed his gavel down again. "I wish there was some other way and I encourage you to find it before this war costs us too much."

"Quiet, spirit! The time for talk has ended," Conchar said turning to exit the room. "The next time we meet blood will flow."

The room faded away and Brendan was left alone in the

darkness with the ghost. He knew he should be terrified, but somehow he knew that the ghost wasn't there to harm him. The hollow companion hovered nearby in silence. Brendan waited, but his peace of mind was growing weary.

"Who are you?" he finally asked the spirit.

The spirit remained impassive and still.

"Are you the Ghost of Christmas Past?"

The spirit smiled and raised an eyebrow. "You could say that." The spirit moved its hand and the places Brendan had been floated past like pages being flipped in a photo album. "What you have seen are events from long ago and now you can do with them as you please."

"Whoa! Wait a minute." Brendan "T-ed" his hands to call time out. "You show me this stuff and then you bail on me? Why did you waste my time?"

"Time? What time have I taken from you?" asked the ghost patiently.

"I don't know. Am I dreaming? Did I eat some bad granola? I don't know what's happening."

"Brendan O'Neal, you have been privy to events not seen for centuries for reasons that I know not. Knowledge is never a waste of time." The spirit floated and considered the human. "You have been chosen by powers that are beyond me."

"But…" began Brendan, but then he stopped. His argument was going to go unheard since the spirit had vanished. As a matter of fact, everything had faded and Brendan found himself leaning his head against the window of the beat up old rental. A string of drool fell onto his shirt when he finally awoke.

Chapter 9
✛ Dullahan ✛

THE OCCUPANTS OF THE BACKSEAT of the car were sleeping peacefully. Lizzie was stretched out and snoozing like it was her comfy mattress from NYC and Rory and Biddy were laid out in the rear window shelf. The front seat was having more trouble resting. Brendan's thoughts lingered on the visions of the past, and that made it hard to relax. He had just had some sort of strange encounter with a spirit, and although he had already seen some freaky stuff, the thought of a ghost still scared him. He also noticed that Dorian was having a tough time sleeping, too. She jostled back and forth in her seat finding no comfort. The view through the tears in the roof weren't that calming, so he took to looking at her instead.

Brendan thought she looked beautiful but troubled. It wasn't her fault that she was a little stressed. Her father being abducted by a griffin was not your average everyday teen issue, after all. When her eyes opened and she looked over at him, he had an urge to tell her about his dream, but thought better of it. What would it matter anyway?

Dorian stretched and squinted to see out of the windshield frame since the glass had been shattered and disposed of after they came to a stop. Brendan took the opportunity to start a conversation. "So, how is it that your father is a Leprechaun and you're not?"

"I am a Leprechaun, Brendan." She yawned and arched her back to stretch out again. "I just choose to be your size sometimes."

Now Brendan knew he was a novice to all of this magic stuff and he was growing more and more curious about it. "But how?" He read Dorian's face and got it. "Oh, magic, of course. How long have Leprechauns been around?"

"Our people have been here for thousands of years."

"Wait, you're a thousand years old?" Brendan's eyes were wide and he was a little freaked by the thought of having a crush on a really old lady.

"No, I'm seventeen, Brendan." She chuckled a little. "We live and die just like you."

"If you're like me, then where does the magic come from?"

"The legend says that a great shadow fell over the world and started an evil and depressing era. After a bunch of suffering and when all hope seemed lost, a brilliant rainbow burst through the dark sky and touched the Earth. The light will always hold the darkness away, and in this case it helped to destroy it. From that day on, the rainbow has given us magic and power, and I guess a sense of protection." Dorian glanced over at Brendan to read his face. He was interested and never once smirked or acted like he didn't believe her. She also noticed his eyes. They were deep and hard to pull away from, but somehow she managed to do so.

"Looks like Morna is trying to bring the dark and scary times back with her griffin and ugly fairies."

"Pretty much," she replied. Dorian shifted her position and leaned her head on her seat's headrest. She found herself staring deeply into Brendan's eyes, and she was hating herself for it. Everything about the moment was tipping towards romantic. The stars were bright, fireflies were glowing, and a song she loved came on the radio.

"I never thanked you for coming along," she said.

They began leaning towards one another, perhaps caught up in the moment, or perhaps fate was beginning to intervene.

"Um, I'm just glad I could help," Brendan replied awkwardly.

They leaned in closer and closer coming within inches of the other's lips. The moment was just about to happen when Brendan's cell phone rang, lighting up like a police car in Paris. Brendan fumbled with it getting the smart phone out of his pocket. He smiled oafishly having had the near blissfulness of a first kiss with Dorian, the most intriguing person he had ever met in his young life, pass by with nothing more than a longing hanging between them.

Lizzie sat bolt-upright in the back seat, groggy and disheveled, and asked, "Whoza? Whatza?"

Brendan turned back to her. "It's just my phone." Seeing that it was his father calling, he answered with the push of a button.

Oscar, who was lying on a lumpy mattress in a slummy hotel smiled at the sound of his son's voice. "Brendan. How are you and Liz?"

A fly walked across his nineteen-inch tube television and nearly got stuck on a large smudge of something that was smeared across the center of the picture.

Brendan glanced back at his sleepy sister and shrugged. "Uh, we're a bit tired. Where are you, Dad?"

Oscar coughed and hacked for a few seconds. "Sorry, it's really smoky in all the buildings I've been in today. I'm in Gilshery." More coughs. "Sorry. I've got this little hotel room––well it's more of a room above a stable–– but its home tonight. Listen, Brendan, I hate leaving you guys alone like this, but I feel like I'm on the verge of a discovery. I'm probably going to be gone a day or two longer than I thought. You kids haven't run out of money yet, have you?"

Brendan sighed in relief. "No, we're fine. Don't worry about us." He was trying to ease his father's mind about feeling guilty. He was also trying to convince him that he and Lizzie were perfectly safe. "Listen, Dad, I better get going. Call me tomorrow, will you?"

"Yeah, okay, Son. I'm really beat, too," Oscar replied. "Love you guys."

Brendan glanced over at Dorian and buckled under the possible embarrassment of telling his father that he loved him. "Us too, Dad. Talk to you tomorrow."

Brendan ended the call and checked the back seat. Lizzie, Rory, and Biddy were sleeping soundly. Their breathing was steady and low and they appeared to be resting quite nicely.

Turning back to Dorian he said, "Now, where were we?"

She was turned away from him, apparently not wanting to listen in on his conversation, but when she replied with only the smallest of snores, he added, "Um, never mind."

Miles away, the ominous pounding of a big and powerful black steed sped towards the sleepy five. The horse's hooves tore divots the size of dinner plates in the dirt road. Its rider was more fearsome than the beast and any animal with half a survival instinct stayed clear. Death would have surely been their fate.

Brendan had finally dozed off and was in the midst of a REM cycle when a shriek from the back seat made him jump. He dismissed it as being a figment of his imagination and turned over towards the window. It wasn't until he felt a small tug on his ear that he fully awakened.

"Brendan, wake up!" shouted Rory.

Brendan turned his head and flung Rory into the driver-side window. The groaning that followed allowed Brendan to spot the ear-tugger.

"What are you doing up, Rory?" asked Brendan.

Rory collected his wits. "We need to get out of here."

Brendan yawned heartily. "We will. Just as soon as first light comes up."

"No!" shouted Rory. "We need to go now!"

Dorian was now stirring. "What's going on, Rory?"

"Something's coming, and it will be here soon," warned Rory.

"What? What's coming?" Dorian was at attention now and stared at the small man.

"Dullahan!" Rory exclaimed, fear rippling through his tiny voice.

Dorian's face echoed Rory's stress and she fell to a pale white.

In the distance, a horse whinnied as if it was Cerberus, the three-headed dog guardian of the Underworld. It was the most terrifying sound that a person could hear, as far as Dorian was concerned. Looking on the hummock ahead, she saw the disturbing silhouette of the ravenous killer, Dullahan.

"You have got to go now!" she shouted in a panic.

Brendan grabbed the key in the ignition and tried to turn the engine over. It sputtered and grinded but it wouldn't start.

"Start, you stupid thing!" he urged.

Dullahan reared his horse back on its hind legs and charged forward. The black stallion covered large chunks of ground with each gallop and everyone in the car could see that the maniac was closing in on them in a hurry.

"Come on! Come on!" shouted Brendan.

Lizzie was up and watching in horror as the dark rider sped toward them. "Who is that guy, anyway?"

"Dullahan," stated Dorian with respect and fear in her tone. "A headless rider that brings death everyplace he goes."

"What's his problem with us?" Lizzie demanded to know, not worrying about the fact that Dorian had mentioned something about a headless rider.

Dorian studied Brendan's technique in starting the car and silently pleaded for the old metal box to respond. "He's one of Morna's minions."

"And he's getting closer by the second, so get this thing going!" added Rory, pointing out of the windshield.

Dullahan surged forward and unsheathed his blade from his back. The metal glinted in the moonlight and sent chills down the spines of the five in the car. The black horse exhaled huge amounts of steam from its large nostrils and its eyes shone red, like fire from the depths of

Hades.

Brendan tried not to focus on his sheer fear and tried the ignition once more. Finally, it turned over.

"Yes!" he exclaimed in triumph as he popped it into gear.

Dullahan was now twenty yards away and the blade had been cocked back, ready to deliver a deathblow. Brendan slammed on the gas and the car lurched forward. He cut the wheel hard right and just escaped the horseman's mighty swipe. Brendan was guiding his beat-up Euro car down the road by the time Dullahan had changed course and took to his pursuit once more.

✦ ✦ ✦

How long had Duncan been Morna's prisoner? The Leprechaun King had to wonder as the seconds crept by and though time was moving slowly, it was hard to keep track of it. The room was dark and musty, like a dungeon would be, with mold and mildew rotting the air.

Duncan leaned against his cage bars and noticed the sweat begin to bead on his forehead. He was both cold and hot at the same time as fever was just beginning to crawl into his body systems. He imagined that he was growing paler by the second, but without a mirror there was no way to confirm it with his eyes. He absently looked over at Wardicon who shook and trembled and resembled a minion from a dark underworld. Was that Duncan's fate? Was that the fate of the Leprechauns?

He heard the clicking of footfalls in the hall beyond the large wood door. Morna entered the room and a bright light nearly blinded Duncan. It took several moments for his eyes to adjust. Once they did, Morna was standing just beyond his cage and one of her goons stood guard at the door.

"Oh, poor, poor, Duncan," began the witch. "You don't look so well." Her grin spoke of her cruelty.

"What have you done to me?" demanded Duncan through a fit of coughs.

Morna laughed the sinister laugh of evil. "You're becoming mine, Duncan, and once I have complete control of you, all of your little, pathetic Leprechauns will be mine as well." She laughed again and studied her prisoner. "But that's not why I'm here. I just wanted to let you know that your daughter did a fine job fending off my Sidhes."

Duncan looked up hopefully at the witch. He began to tremble slightly with his transformation well underway.

"Honestly, she did do a great job, so that's why I sent Dullahan to say hello."

The Leprechaun King's bloodshot eyes opened in recognition. His head shook numbly in denial.

"Don't worry, Duncan, by this time tomorrow you won't even care if she lived or died."

Morna turned on her heels and strode out of the dungeon. Her deranged cackles echoed through the halls for several agonizing minutes. Duncan hung his head as a single tear rolled down his cheek and through his beard. He couldn't help but feel that all hope was lost.

✦ ✦ ✦

Dullahan had caught up to the straining car. He slashed at the back end with his heavy blade and tore through the back bumper causing it to rip away in shreds. Lizzie, Rory, and Biddy moved up as far as possible, clinging to the backs of the front seats.

"Can't this hunk of junk go any faster?" screamed Lizzie.

"I'm trying!" Brendan checked the rearview mirror and finally got a good look at Dullahan. The headless part was dead-on accurate. This guy had nothing where his head and neck should have been. He wore dark clothing and had a flowing cape that looked alive. The horse was almost as frightening simply because of its size. Although, the fiery red eyes didn't make Brendan want to ask for a ride.

"Blast him, Dorian!"

Dorian shook her head. "I'm not that powerful, Brendan! This is an evil being from its creation, and the Sidhe's weren't."

"Well, thanks for the history lesson," Brendan replied in frustration.

The side of the road was alive, if one can use that word to describe what lay in wait in the brush, with a pair of pearl-white eyes of smoke. They narrowed as they watched the car rush by with the fool demon, Dullahan, in hot pursuit. The order was given to stay away, to stay out of these affairs, but to stand by the wayside seemed unnatural. It would be a crime not to get involved.

The headless maniac hacked at the trunk of the car

with his blade. The sound of the sword slicing through the trunk was terrifying. Lizzie screamed, but the others had voices that couldn't make any sound. After another slash, the trunk flew off its hinges in two pieces. Dullahan and his black monster of a horse stayed in stride as they rode right in between the severed parts.

Brendan was beginning to grow desperate and his mind was flooded with panic. It was hard to think clearly and consider a best-case solution. He was coming up with nothing over and over again and the sound of his sister's cries made the situation that much worse for him.

He finally decided on something crazy. "Dorian, take the wheel!"

Dorian, who looked lost and scared in the passenger seat focused her eyes on Brendan. "What? What are you going to do?"

"Just take the wheel!" he yelled.

She read his eyes and knew that there was no way to deter his thinking. She slid over his lap and placed her foot on the accelerator and grabbed the steering wheel. Satisfied that she was in control of the car, he slid into the passenger seat.

As Brendan turned his head he saw the big, frightening headless guy jump from his horse and land in the trunk space. Brendan's eyes were wrought with terror as the evil thing lifted his sword into the air and became primed to strike down on Lizzie.

Something in Brendan snapped. There was no way that he was going to let this freak show hurt his sister.

"NOOOOO!" he called out in mid-air as he leapt from the front seat and slammed into the evil demon.

Dorian saw the whole moment as if it were in slow-motion. Brendan's body had glided through the air like a torpedo and he speared Dullahan with such force that the two of them toppled out of the trunk and into the night air.

In mid-flight Brendan could hardly believe that he had done what he had done. All he knew at that moment was that he wanted Dullahan to hit the ground first. He used his leverage and angled the monster's back and shoulders directly towards the hard road. When they hit the ground Brendan still felt an enormous impact even with Dullahan on the bottom. The air was instantly gone from his lungs and he was seeing stars as the pair began to roll after contact with the road.

"Brendan!" Lizzie screamed as she reached into the night after her brother.

Dorian was so surprised by his heroic actions that it took her a few seconds to realize she needed to stop and go back for him. Part of her was thinking that it was already too late for Brendan. In her mind if the fall didn't kill him then the headless horseman would. In spite of her instinct to just keep going, she slammed on the brakes and cut the wheel. The car drifted and they faced opposite of the direction that would have probably led to safety. She mashed down the gas pedal and headed back for Brendan.

Brendan was hurting all over. It felt like the entire football team had just used him for tackling practice.

His vision was spotted with stars and hearts and clovers. He attributed that to the fact that he was in Ireland and his favorite cereal was still Lucky Charms. He pulled his upper half up to a sitting position and put his hand to his head. He noticed that he had a gash somewhere in his hair and a small amount of blood was trickling out. He had other cuts and he was sure to be bruised, but nothing felt broken or too mangled, so he was counting himself lucky.

He spotted Dullahan some twelve feet away lying on his back. He wasn't moving but being a movie buff like he was, Brendan knew that it didn't mean anything. Right on queue, Dullahan sat bolt upright and spun his way to his feet. He turned and began to stalk towards Brendan with his sword in hand. The demon reached to his belt and pulled an ax free of its loop as well. Brendan imagined that the evil guy would probably be giving him a really evil look at the moment since he did just knock him off of a moving car, but the fact was the guy didn't have a head. Even so, Dullahan didn't need to give any intimidating looks. The moving body without the use of a head was intimidating enough. Throw in the sword and an ax and he was downright bone-chilling.

Brendan backed away in a crab-walk as the demon slashed down with his sword. The blade gashed the road in between Brendan's legs.

"Whoa!" he exclaimed. "Can't we talk about this?"

Dullahan yanked the sword from the road. "No," echoed a voice from deep with his chest cavity.

That word was the absolute worst sound Brendan

had ever heard. He had heard that word a ton in his lifetime from his dad and his teachers and from girls that he had asked out, but this was different. It was like the devil himself was speaking to him and that was not a conversation that he wanted to have.

Dullahan slammed his blade down again and Brendan had managed to roll to the left and to safety. He got to his feet quickly and the two stood "looking" at each other. Dullahan let the moment hang and then he began to make strides toward the young American.

Bam!

Dorian let out a war cry as she steered the beat up little rental over the evil demon. The crunch was sickening as the car impacted Dullahan. He was smashed to the ground as the car continued to roll over him. His body was dragged for twenty feet before Dorian had managed to bring the car to a screeching halt.

Brendan limped over to the car. When he got there everyone had a rush of relief except for Dorian. She was still gripping the wheel with a death-lock causing her knuckles to whiten.

"Are you all okay?" Brendan asked.

Lizzie had tears in her eyes as she leapt from the back seat and wrapped her brother in a lung-constricting hug. "I can't believe you did that!"

Brendan held her at arm's length. "Like I'm going to let some headless dork hurt my sister."

She hugged him again as Dorian stepped out of the car. "That headless dork is a minion of pure evil. For centuries he's ridden this land and has left death in his wake."

"Well, not any more," chuckled Brendan. "Looks like the twenty-first century caught up to him."

Dorian shook her head. "It's not that simple, Brendan. Evil is really hard to kill."

Dullahan must have been a fan of the horror genre too, because at that moment he thrust his sword up through the middle of the little car. With one sweeping motion he sliced the car in half like he was cutting lemons. The violent action sent Biddy and Rory flying as the two halves of the vehicle were launched through the air.

Lizzie screamed and retreated behind Brendan. Dullahan rose to his full height, which was substantial considering he was headless, and let out a guttural yell.

"You've got to be kidding me!" Brendan said in frustration.

"See," said Dorian. She looked at the demon with hate in her heart. He was part of something that started this whole adventure and now her father's life hung in the balance. She was angry, but she felt helpless to do anything about it. Now this maniac was about to kill them and all she could do was wait for it to happen.

She knitted her brow and decided to go out fighting. She began to blast the demon with golden energy, only causing him to pause in amusement. The moment passed and he strode forward now taking to deflecting her blasts with his gleaming blade.

Brendan, Lizzie, and Dorian were backing up with every stride Dullahan took.

"Got any other ideas?" Brendan asked.

"I think this is our last stand," Dorian replied between blasts.

Brendan grabbed a branch from a nearby tree and stepped to the front. "You guys run for it. I'll buy you some time."

"No!" screeched Lizzie. "We're not leaving you!"

Brendan raised his stick and readied himself for an onslaught from Dullahan when he spotted a strange sight. A pair of smoke-like eyes floated in behind the dark and scary killer and hovered.

Dullahan must have sensed a presence behind him because he turned and raised his sword. "Gorgoch!" the demon bellowed.

Dullahan was hoisted into the air by some unseen force. His sword fell to the ground like a lawn dart and stuck. The demon dangled momentarily before a voice on the wind cried, "Dullahan!"

The horseman was then launched miles away like a rocket. Seconds later his demon horse could be seen galloping after his defeated rider, and the sword faded out of existence.

Chapter 10

✛ Gorgoch ✛

WHAT JUST HAPPENED?" asked Lizzie.

No one blamed her for her confusion. Brendan was oblivious to what just took place, too. One minute they were about to die at the hand of a headless guy and the next the evil killer was flying through the air, sent a whole lot of miles away. Brendan was ready to chalk it up to a miracle until Dorian smiled.

"Gorgoch?" she said softly. "Is that you?"

The smoky eyes came into existence and appeared twenty feet above their heads. After the eyes, other features started to blink into reality until a twenty-five foot tall man was standing before them. Brendan and Lizzie jumped backwards.

"Great, we go from one small bad guy to a giant one," said Brendan, his stick held like a baseball bat.

The giant spirit-man turned into a wisp of smoke and then reformed as a normal, average, everyday-sized man. Most of his giant form drifted away on the breeze.

"What are you doing so far from Corways, Dorian?" the spirit asked.

Dorian's smile faded as quickly as it had come and reached over and gave the spirit a hug. The spirit solidified himself for the briefest of moments and held her in his arms, leaving Brendan amazed, confused, and jealous all at the same time.

"Morna stole my father, Gorgoch," began Dorian as she pulled out of the embrace. "I'm not sure what she's playing at."

Brendan cleared his throat to draw a little attention. "What, you know this guy?"

"Of course, I do," Dorian said smiling again. "Brendan and Lizzie O'Neal, meet Gorgoch."

The spirit man extended his hand and solidified his body once again. Brendan and Lizzie both shook it. Brendan could tell that Lizzie was a little grossed out, but she didn't say anything. She just had a weird nostril-flaring look on her face.

"You can call me Artair," said Gorgoch with a shimmering smile.

Lizzie shrugged. "Hi, Artie. I'm Lizzie."

"I'm very pleased to meet you," Gorgoch replied.

Brendan tried not to stare at the guy, but it was hard. It would be for anyone. This was a real life ghost that you could interact with and even shake hands and converse with. Brendan tried to study the guy's features, but it was difficult. It was like trying to look at an image underwater as the sun shone on the surface. His features were elusive all except for the eyes. They were completely white like smoke trapped in a flashlight beam.

"Thanks for all of your concern about us."

Brendan turned back to spot Biddy and Rory climbing free of some bushes.

"Sure the car we were in was just torn to bits, but we're fine," Rory said with obvious sarcasm.

"No need to worry about us, now is there?" piped up Biddy.

Dorian cringed. "Sorry, we were just a little preoccupied with our guest." She nodded towards Gorgoch.

"Oh, looky there, Rory. It's Gorgoch," said Biddy.

"Great timing, Artair," joked Rory. "Did you have to wait until our only transportation was destroyed?"

Gorgoch shrugged. "I'm into the dramatic, I suppose."

The five and Gorgoch found a fallen tree trunk to sit on and after a few minutes of small talk Gorgoch turned back to the heavy issue at hand.

"Now, tell me about what Morna is up to."

✦ ✦ ✦

A small stone shack was alive with the nightlife of Gilshery. The chimney was covered in soot and the wood shingles were badly in need of repair, but anyone who wished to enjoy a pint and fellowship with friends was at the tiny pub. That included about twenty night owls and farmers and Oscar O'Neal with his new friend, Charlie.

Oscar enjoyed seeing the fine people of Gilshery out and about and experiencing life. They had worked hard that day doing whatever it was that they did and deserved a nice relaxing time with friends. Oscar liked to think that they had worked hard and deserved the break, but that's how he was. He was a glass-half-full kind of guy and that's how he was approaching his current project. Sure it was partly research for the university who had given him the grant, but it was also a chance to find out more about his family's history. He wished that the kids could see that and how much it meant to him. Maybe one day they would understand.

"Ah, the nightlife in Gilshery. Probably reminds you of New York," joked Charlie.

Charlie and Oscar found a table in a corner and ordered up a round. Coffee for Oscar, who was "on duty" and a draft for Charlie who wasn't.

"So, you were saying that the search finally took a turn for the better?"

Oscar smiled broadly as he explained his unbelievable

luck at the records room back in Galway. Charlie seemed to be surprised by the luck as well.

"So you know about me, Charlie. What do you do?"

Charlie took a large gulp to finish the glass. "I am a jeweler." He produced a charm from his pocket and held it out for Oscar.

"Its beautiful. What is it?"

"You can call it a Celtic Knot."

Oscar turned the charm over in his fingers and examined it. It looked like three outlines of thin leaves laid out so that the ends toward the middle overlapped or crossed. It was beautiful craftsmanship and took the work of a real artist.

"Folklore says that it represents the crossing of our inner spirituality and our physical beings."

Oscar admired it for a moment longer and then attempted to hand it back to Charlie.

Charlie held his hand up. "You keep it, friend. Think of it as a welcome to Ireland gift." Charlie got to his feet just as the waitress arrived. He leaned in and whispered something in her ear before he laid down a group of folded Euros on the waitress's tray.

His face was glowing in a bright blue light from his laptop screen and it vastly contrasted the soft glow coming out of the lanterns randomly placed around the pub. A large mug, empty except for the foam that rung the bottom of the glass, sat idly next to two others on Oscar's table.

"Have a great night, Oscar. Good luck on your

research." Charlie left with a tip of his cap.

Two hours later, the waitress approached his table and laid another drink down at his table.

"Um, how many did he pay for?"

"All he said was 'as many as it takes,'" she replied with a grin.

He returned her smile with one of his own.

"I hope you are enjoying your night," she said.

"I am," he hiccupped. "I am on a mission, you see."

"Is that so?" The waitress raised a curious brow.

"It is so." Oscar lifted his mug and took a small sip. "I am trying to find my ancestry here in your town."

"Well, what have you found out so far?"

He tilted the laptop screen so she could see. "Not much. But I am determined and I shall not fail."

"A lot of Yanks come here in search of their family tree. Most are just searching for something. What are you hoping to find?"

Oscar tilted his head. "I guess I have just always felt a pull to come to Ireland. It's like a feeling that you can never get rid of until you act on it."

"Well, I hope you find everything you're searching for." She left him to his work and his draft.

He thought a little longer on his motives and found that he still really couldn't explain it, but it felt stronger than ever at that moment. He glanced down at the Knot charm and thought he saw something move within its metal, but glancing over at the empty mugs satisfied his question.

✦ ✦ ✦

Duncan's mind was foggy when he tried to think, but in the moments where he quieted his thoughts, the images he had were clear and frightening. Morna was invading his brain, and he was losing control. He wondered how much longer he would be able to fend her off and preserve his conscious mind. Looking at Wardicon, he could see what the results would be if he couldn't defend his consciousness. It would be pain and misery and the worst part was that it would be his people that would suffer the most. He was responsible for them and for keeping their magic. It was he that would be responsible for handing over that power and their lives to Morna.

Even with all of those thoughts playing at his mind and all of the images that Morna had implanted in her attempt to crush his will and seize total control, one thought helped to keep his mind his own.

"Dorian," he mumbled as thunder clashed somewhere outside the castle and far beyond his prison.

✦ ✦ ✦

Dorian had retold the story to Gorgoch while Lizzie, Rory, Biddy, and Brendan filled in the gaps when they thought that she was leaving something out. After thirty minutes or so Gorgoch seemed to grasp the concept.

"So, that's all you know?" began Gorgoch. "You don't know if it is truly Morna's bidding that the Sidhes and Dullahan were doing?"

"All I have to go on is my gut, Artie, and besides, I

had once seen Morna with that same griffin." She looked directly into Gorgoch's fluid features. "I would bet a pot of gold that she's behind it all."

"Well, I can't say for certain if she is or if she's not, but I am willing to take you as far as the shore for you to find out." Gorgoch scratched his head. "I wouldn't put it past the old witch, that I know for certain."

"Why only the shore?" asked Brendan. "A big guy like you could really come in handy when things get rough again."

Gorgoch let his head drop slightly. "She's the reason I'm in this state of being. She killed me in life and took control of my spirit to do her evil. I escaped after doing horrible things, so I don't plan on giving her another chance."

Dorian looked around at the others. "Then its settled. Gorgoch will take us as far as the coast and then we can take a ship to Scotland."

"Well, I think its cool and all that Artie here is going to escort us to the shore, but it's going to be a long walk," observed Brendan.

"Who said anything about walking?" asked Dorian giving a sly nod toward Gorgoch. The old spirit's smile was very clear beneath the shimmering appearance of his face.

✦ ✦ ✦

"I can't believe we're doing this!" Brendan yelled as the wind rushed past his ears.

He glanced around and saw the faces of his traveling companions and only Lizzie's expression reflected his own. They were all clinging to an expanded Gorgoch who apparently was able to fly. Brendan saw no logic in what was currently happening, but what he learned in recent history helped him to not question it too much. Why wouldn't a ghost be able to expand his body and soar through the air with five of the living on his back? Seriously, why not?

Lizzie was apparently not ready to accept it as she looked through Gorgoch's transparent body at the landscape passing quickly beneath them and had to ask. "Now, why aren't we plunging to our deaths again?"

Rory, who was closest to Lizzie and Brendan, answered. "Gorgoch is half-spirit and half-man, which means he exists in both our world and in the next."

"I'll say it," said Lizzie. "This is just crazy. Just flat-out crazy."

"Okay, okay. We get it, Liz. It's crazy," replied Brendan, still not really believing his eyes either. "Well, I'm glad it's the middle of the night at least."

"Why?" asked Dorian, a puzzled look on her face.

"Could you imagine looking up and seeing all of us soaring over your head on a nearly transparent guy?"

"Of course I could," Dorian replied. "I'm taking advantage of his fancy flying powers right now, aren't I?"

Brendan rolled his eyes. "Believe me, normal people would be freaking out right now."

Dorian smiled to herself, admiring Brendan as the wind passed through his hair.

Riding "Gorgoch Air" was the strangest experience of

Brendan's life. Considering the last couple of days, that was saying something. He had to hand it to the dead guy, though, because the flight was comfortable and after getting over the initial shock of what they were doing, it was really exciting. Ireland was absolutely beautiful, even with little light to see. The skies were clear and breezy and the first stars were beginning to dot the night sky. He imagined that this was the feeling that hang gliders got as they took to the air.

The massive ghost plane made the travel time considerably shorter than if they were driving, and the group reached the coast only after a short while. Brendan didn't time it or think too much about it since he had other things on his mind. Things like Dorian's smile and Dorian's eyes and Dorian's hair and so on and so on... Also he was trying to not think about the rental car that was just annihilated by the headless freak show.

The only time the car even came up in conversation was when Lizzie asked, "What do you think Dad's going to say about the car?"

All Brendan could do was shrug. "It's going to be hard to explain this one."

Lizzie smiled, "I bet we don't get the deposit back either."

They laughed together for the first time in awhile. Neither one wanted to think about what surprises lay in wait.

Gorgoch landed with the grace of a swan and gently placed his passengers on the ground. He shrank himself back to the height of an average-sized man.

"Here we are," he announced.

Dorian nodded, but wasted no time. "I'll go and secure us a boat." With that she walked away in the direction of a decrepit, old, tin-paneled shack. The lights were on and an "Open" sign blinked in the window.

Brendan watched her knock, then wait for a few moments before the rusty metal door swung open and she stepped inside. He turned to Gorgoch.

"Thanks for the ride, but I still wish you'd come with us. We could really use you."

Gorgoch shook his head sadly. "I don't think you really want that."

"Why?" asked Lizzie.

"If the witch can take control of me again then there's no telling how much evil she'd make me do." Gorgoch stared off into the night, his features elusive. "I don't want to go back there again."

"So, what's the story anyway?" Lizzie inquired.

"It's a long, boring tale and I wouldn't want to waste your time with it."

Rory cleared his throat. "Basically, our ghostly friend was in love with a Scottish girl and … "

Gorgoch interrupted. "That's enough, Rory." Gorgoch looked at the others. "Long story short, Morna saw an opportunity to cause havoc and she did. Please tell Dorian goodbye."

As Gorgoch walked away, Brendan could feel the sadness in the air as if it were a physical presence—like a blanket of misery was blown off of a clothes line.

Biddy hopped on top of a distraught and wobbly picnic table and stared out after the ghost. Gorgoch turned to vapor and drifted away. "It's a sad tale, really." The little Leprechaun sighed. "Morna sent her little crony, Dullahan, out to maim and cause a large raucous in a small town."

Brendan shook his head. What was Morna's problem? The vision he had came to the forefront of his mind again. He remembered how angry the wizard was at that meeting. Perhaps that was the way wizards and witches really were: more Lord Voldemort than Harry Potter. He caught a few more of Biddy's words and focused back on the conversation.

"... leaving that town in disarray. He burned half the barns and sent those poor folks running. The headless git even killed six people," Biddy said angrily.

"Let me guess, Artie's wife was among the dead," Lizzie deduced.

"Actually, they weren't married just yet," added Rory. "I think that blessed event was still a week away."

"Enraged by what had happened and with a heart set on revenge, Artie followed Dullahan back to Morna's castle." Biddy laughed at the absurdness of the idea of following the homicidal maniac back to the witch's castle. "Somehow, he found a way in."

"You have got to be kidding me?" Brendan asked in disbelief.

"Artie was persistent, he was." Biddy recalled. "He ran

into the witch's forest and … "

"And," Lizzie prodded after a pause.

"Before he could take his revenge, the witch had trapped him. He was only human, after all," said Biddy.

"The old witch laughed at him and his pain," she continued after a brief pause. "And then she cast a spell on him that was so potent that it killed him."

"Well, at least half of him. That half gave him a connection to the spirit world where his living half kept his connection to this world." Rory looked back and forth between Lizzie and Brendan, the sadness stinging his eyes.

"Ewwww," Lizzie added with a sour face.

Biddy chuckled a little. "The witch seized control of our friend and forced him to do terrible things, only she didn't count on the human side of him to resist her will. She didn't count on him to break free."

"That's how he ended up in Ireland," concluded Rory.

"And that good, human side of him is what Morna hates most of all about humanity," Biddy said in a rush. "I feel like she won't stop until she has destroyed the humans and all of the magicks as well."

They were silent for a few moments before Brendan spoke. "She couldn't stop Gorgoch, could she?"

Rory and Biddy looked up, tears poised to fall from the corners of Biddy's eyes. "No, she couldn't," she replied.

"He even goes around and does all these nice things for the living," added Rory. "Usually where Dullahan is causing a problem."

"You see? She hasn't won anything yet," Brendan declared. "So don't give up on us. Don't give up on our mission. We'll stop her no matter what."

Dorian was standing at a distance listening in on the conversation. She knew she had judged Brendan too harshly before and that she should have listened to Biddy. Biddy was always right about people. Listening to him and his confidence in the team made her so proud to have him along. It made her feelings for him that much stronger and harder to resist. She needed to remain focused and clouding the journey with a fog-headed romance could do nothing but put the team in jeopardy. She decided to admire Brendan and respect him, but that was it. Those other feelings would have to wait, no matter how strong they were growing.

She walked up with her bag slung over her shoulder and asked, "Where's Gorgoch?"

Biddy piped up first. "He left on the wind."

Dorian knitted her brow in frustration and reached into her bag and held out a small pint of cream. "I guess I'll give this to an alley cat, then."

"Okay," said Brendan in confusion. "Why would you have cream?"

"Gorgoch is usually rewarded with a jug of cream," explained Rory. "I prefer two percent milk myself."

Lizzie shook her head. "You people are weird."

"Did you get us a boat?" Brendan asked, trying to get the mission back on track.

Dorian nodded. "It's right over there." She pointed to

the bay where an old, rickety boat bobbed on the water. It looked like an old Viking ship only it was badly in need of repairs and a new coat of paint.

Brendan pointed out the concern on the others' faces. "That's the boat? You know they have made boats in the last two-hundred years, right?"

Dorian allowed a smile. "True, but this is the one we need. Its captain is special."

Moments later an old, crotchety man hobbled out of the tiny shack. He relied on his cane for balance, but Brendan wasn't too confident in the old-timer's ability to stand even with the cane at his disposal.

"You're kidding me, right?" asked Brendan, leaning in close to Dorian.

Rory and Biddy were showing no signs of displeasure at the choice of captain. Instead they charged forward and greeted the old man by yelling, "Sean!"

Sean, the Viking boat captain, smiled wide with a nearly toothless grin. The name stirred something in Brendan's memory, a familiarity of sorts. He had seen this man somewhere, but he couldn't place where.

"Rory! Biddy! It's good to see you again," Sean greeted them back.

"Uncle Sean, this is Brendan and Lizzie O'Neal," said Dorian.

Sean shook Lizzie's hand and then Brendan's, but he stared deep into the young American's eyes. Brendan got a sense of recognition from the old man, as well. "O'Neal, you say? Hmmmm. Well, welcome aboard."

Chapter 11

✝ Merrows ✝

LOOKING AROUND THE DECK of the *Clair*, Brendan began to worry. It was like stepping onto an already sunken boat with its barnacles, warped floor planks, and rusted bands and eyehooks. Brendan didn't know much about boats, but he recognized that this ship was not one he would want to be sailing on. The deck was a mess with beer cans and chip bags settled into nooks and rotted out deck chairs thrown askew without the hope of luring a rear end.

It was odd that Dorian would want to take this heap across the channel, but it was even more odd to him that he seemed to be the only one who looked concerned. For a moment he had thought that Lizzie might be sharing his opinion, but after considering it for a moment he just assumed that she was only grossed out.

Brendan was standing next to Dorian. He leaned in and said, "Uh, are you sure about this? I mean, I still got that money my dad left for me."

Dorian raised her eyebrow and smiled. "We don't need money for this boat, silly."

"No kidding," Brendan replied sarcastically. "But we may need tetanus shots when we're done with this trip."

Lizzie nodded, but Dorian just ignored him. She strolled over to her uncle and placed her bag on a wobbly table.

"The payment is in there, I assume," Sean said, angling his eyes towards the bag.

Dorian nodded. She reached in and pulled out an odd assortment of items. Brendan and Lizzie looked at each other with confused glances. She laid the leather-bound book from the village on the table. It had seen better days, but the binding was still holding up. She also placed a soup ladle down with a clank. Brendan allowed his eyes to travel from the ladle to Sean and a small twinkle shown in the old man's eyes. The last item was a small baggie filled with maroon-colored roots.

"This is all I have, Sean," said Dorian.

Sean looked the items over once more and scrunched up his face. "I need the iodine to make it work, deary."

Lizzie perked up. "Iodine? Wait a tick." She reached into her own bag and dug around for a moment. She pulled out a small brown bottle and held it aloft. "Will this do?"

Sean took the bottle and examined it. He opened it up and took in a large whiff. He grinned a gummy grin and nodded. "Should do just fine."

"What do you need all that stuff for?" Brendan asked, looking at the junk on the table.

Sean motioned for the group to follow him. He hobbled the length of the boat until he reached the helm. Perched on a thin table was a small cauldron. Sean added the roots and the iodine to an already boiling concoction and used the ladle to stir it around. "We need a little energy to get this old boat going."

"And the book contains the spell that makes it all work?" asked Brendan.

Sean chuckled. "No, I loaned the book to Duncan and Dorian was nice enough to bring it back to me." The old man held it up revealing the title.

Brendan read it. "*Twilight?*" He couldn't believe it. "You're kidding, right?"

Sean shrugged. "It's a good book."

Sean reached down and retrieved a lid from a shelf beneath the table and covered the pot. For a few seconds they all stood in silence, waiting on something to happen. The lid began to rattle like a stovetop pot that was threatening to boil over. As the lid shook rays of golden light streaked out and illuminated the group. Seconds more ticked by and Brendan found that he was holding his breath. He forced himself to inhale. The lid shook so much that it was no longer covering the pot. It was raised into the air by the golden energy that was fighting to free itself from the container.

Brendan began to step back, but Dorian reached down and took his hand. Looking at her, he could see that she was smiling, so he trusted her. He realized that he was would trust her no matter what.

The light from the pot dimmed and gave way to a golden mist that leaked out of the cauldron. The mist spread out from the pot and drifted over the deck and up the mast and encased every part of the ship. It was a truly unreal sight. Brendan found his own smile.

Sean chuckled and squinted in the light of the mist. "Next stop, Port Hegles."

The ship glowed and shimmered with amazing magic as it pulled away from port. Brendan noticed an odd stillness and as it dawned on him that he couldn't feel the wind, something even crazier happened. The ship slowly sank into the water. As the water level rose around the boat, Brendan and the others began to panic.

"We're going down!" shouted Lizzie.

"Hold on," soothed Sean. "Relax."

The water splashed higher and higher and eventually

sprayed against the golden mist that encased the ship. Watching the water land against the golden dome reminded Brendan of being at an aquarium and walking beneath the shark tanks. Soon enough the entire ship was beneath the water.

Brendan shook his head. He leaned in close to Dorian. "Okay. I take it back. This ship is pretty cool."

"See?" she responded.

"See what?" Brendan said curiously.

"Oh, just that I'm always right," she said with a sly grin.

The group watched as the dark sea became partially lit by the golden mist and a few floodlights that popped to life. Out of the corner of Brendan's eye he could see that Sean was watching him. He didn't know if that was good or bad, but he was sure that he would find out soon.

✦ ✦ ✦

Duncan looked like a man, or Leprechaun, that was on death's doorstep. Whatever Morna was doing to him made him feel like he had the plague. He was sweating and wheezing. He felt clammy and had moments of hot flashes that nearly knocked him unconscious. He was slouched against a bar, defeated and weak. He barely glanced up when Morna and Dullahan entered the room.

"My, don't we have a little resilient search party after us?" Morna said with disdain apparent in her voice. She observed Duncan and knew that the old Leprechaun couldn't hold out much longer.

"You know, they have turned out to be more troublesome than I anticipated. Even Dullahan failed to stop them." The witch shot a stare at the headless demon that made him slink away into the shadows. Duncan only looked up at his captor, but she could see that small glimmer of hope in his eyes. That last frail bit of hope was always the hardest to kill, but she had been successful at it in the past.

"But even now they tarry onward towards my castle, the fools. They've even taken to the sea for passage, no doubt feeling a bit safer." Morna laughed.

Duncan continued to stare at her but said nothing. She leaned close like a friend about to share a secret. "It's a false sense of safety, my old friend. I can assure you of that."

Duncan wheezed.

"I'm going to give them to my Merrows."

Duncan showed a small amount of confusion with a slight change in his expression, but he couldn't vocalize it. Behind Morna, two of her minions entered the dungeon pushing a large aquatic tank. They shoved it across the room unceremoniously and stood in the doorway like intimidating statues. The tank slammed into the walls and water sloshed over the top. A dark figure bobbed in the water.

"I believe you know Usis, the Merrow Queen," Morna introduced them as if she were hosting a party.

Duncan pulled on the bars and tilted his head to look over at Usis. The Merrow queen was apparently none too pleased with being thrown around and she lashed out at the glass walls of her prison. Duncan grew even more depressed as he watched her contorted features press against the glass. She was normally so beautiful and enchanting. Duncan remembered being so enamored with her that he halfway considered asking for her hand in marriage. But now Usis's skin had lost its color and her hands were like talons of the griffin, sharp and jagged. Her hair, which normally flowed and enthralled was now stark white and brittle. She bared her teeth at the room and Duncan saw that they were pointed and broken. He slumped back down and looked back to Morna.

"And I thought she was beautiful before," Morna turned to exit the room but looked back to Duncan just before she hit the threshold. "I'll let you know how it turns out. I'm sure you two want to catch up on old times."

✦ ✦ ✦

The ship was moving along quite smoothly beneath the sea. Brendan looked past the golden dome that sheltered them from the crushing pressure of the water. Though all the others except for Lizzie were already over the splendor of the crazy magic, Brendan was still amazed.

Lizzie, Rory, and Biddy were near the helm while Sean was leaning on his cane with one hand and steering the ship with the other. He was happy to see Lizzie smile. They had already been through so much that he was worried about his kid sister. He also knew that they had been really lucky to this point. Irish luck perhaps?

He let his gaze fall back down to the angel on his right. Dorian had an old, ancient-looking map on her lap that must have been made in the sixteen hundreds. He glanced over her shoulder and saw that it was a map of Scotland. He spotted Port Hegles and then saw a red circle around a place called Louseen.

"What's in Louseen?" he asked.

"That's where Morna's castle is according to Gorgoch." She was biting her lip in concentration and Brendan couldn't help but think that it made her all that more appealing. Her hair was hanging down in her face except for a part that she had swept behind her ear. It framed her profile in such a way that Brendan couldn't help but stare longingly at her.

"Well, when we get to Port Hegles we'll need to rent a car and then move as fast as we … " she stopped when she looked up at Brendan. "Were you just checking me out?" She smiled.

Brendan was caught and he knew it, but he denied it anyway. "What? No, I was … what?"

Dorian laughed at his verbal bumbling.

"Why would I want to… you know?" he said in his defense.

"Are you saying that I'm not worth checking out?" she asked him with a pseudo-hurt look.

"No, just the opposite," he back peddled. "You're gorgeous."

She continued to smile, and that was contagious. He smiled and they began to lean in for a kiss. Brendan's heart pounded at the prospect of touching his lips to hers. Closer and closer they moved, their breath mixing between them. He closed his eyes and then… nothing.

His lips meet empty space.

He opened one eye to check to she if she hadn't bailed on him, and he saw that she was still there. Her attention wasn't on him any longer, though. He followed her gaze and saw a few dark shapes outside of the golden dome.

"What are they?" Dorian asked in wondering.

Brendan knew what they were. He remembered seeing those shapes in the water during his little trip under the sea. "I think they are Merrows."

Sean was limping down a wooden staircase and grunted his agreement. "Aye, but this water is not usually on their traveling course."

Lizzie was leaning over the railing to listen in on the conversation. Truth be known, she wanted to find out if Brendan was finally going to lay one on Dorian or not, but that little drama would have to wait for another time. For now, she was more concerned with the dark shadows. "What are Merrows again?"

Rory was perched on the wheel. "I don't know what you call them, but they are people with fish bodies."

"Oh, like mermaids," smiled Lizzie.

Biddy was standing on the wheel as well. She nodded. "I've heard of mermaids and they are one and the same."

"Which is fine by me since Merrows are a peaceful lot," Rory said, a bit of relief in his voice.

Brendan was still feeling a little on edge about any of the so-called mythical beings he had met. "Remember the fairies were supposed to be peaceful."

"Sidhes," Dorian said, correcting him.

"Whatever," shrugged Brendan. "Point is—they might be under Morna's control, too."

The tension was high beneath the dome. They all seemed to be holding their collective breath as more and more of the shadows swam outside of the golden shield. Lizzie spotted one hovering ten feet to her left. She cautiously walked to the dome to get a better look at the Merrow.

The Merrow flitted its tail and its arms to stay in place and then gradually came forward. Lizzie was having a hard time seeing through the dome, but she was getting a fuzzy outline. It was sort of like trying to look at Gorgoch in the face.

Lizzie had an image in her head, though. Flowing red hair, shimmering green tail, and a wonderful singing voice were the only things she could picture.

"Aren't you just a pretty thing?" Lizzie cooed.

The Merrow appeared to respond by doing a somersault before coming even closer. Lizzie squinted her eyes and held her hand up against the dome to try and get a better look. When the Merrow did the same, Lizzie's eyes grew wide with terror.

The Merrow bared her fangs and tensed her body to show its angry aggression towards the travelers. She let out an impossibly high-pitched scream that caused everyone within the dome to cover their ears.

"Shut up!" Lizzie yelled.

The Merrow revealed a silver dagger and reared her arm back with the blade glinting with a golden reflection.

She drove the blade into the golden dome as if it were made of cloth. The Merrow screamed and tore hard at the incision. More ugly Merrows slammed into the dome and sliced into it as well.

"Get us to the surface, Sean!" Dorian commanded.

Sean was already on his way to the cauldron. "I don't have to be told twice," he replied.

He reached out and touched the cold iron and closed his eyes. Water started to spray in from the rips in the dome. The terrible Merrows clawed and gnashed their teeth attempting to shred the protection away from their prey.

"Better hurry, Sean!" Brendan yelled over the screech of the Merrows that was now at a deafening decibel.

A few Merrows had managed to tug and pull at the magic barrier and create enough space for their bodies to fit through. Dorian was quick, though, and blasted them back into the sea with golden bursts from her palms. Water continued to pour in from the shredded dome. Other Merrows also took the opportunity to take a crack at getting inside, but Dorian was able to blast them away as well.

Sea water poured in on the travelers and made keeping a good footing nearly impossible. Dorian was blasting away while Brendan took to swinging an oar from the life boat. He stood near one tear and felt like he was playing whack-a-mole. A Merrow would stick its head in through the tear and Brendan would smash an oar into its face. He counted points in his head.

"Come on, Sean!" Dorian stressed in between magical blasts. "We're taking on too much water!"

Sean was sweaty and covered in sea salt, but when he opened his eyes no one doubted his will power. They glowed and matched the dome in luster. His cane fell to the deck as he touched the cauldron with both hands. More and more water spewed onto the deck and thousands of Merrows advanced on the ship.

The sea was calm and serene in the hour before sunrise. A soft wind licked at the surface of the water and a few gulls circled overhead in the hopes of finding a little breakfast. Suddenly, a tattered old ship burst from the water, a golden dome dissipating in the morning air. Many Merrows clung to the boat as it emerged and settled on the surface.

Lizzie was soaked and nearly exhausted. She was near the railing when she noticed a gray-skinned claw dug into the wood. She slowly got to her feet and sneaked to the side. Looking over, she saw dozens and dozen of Merrows climbing their way to the top.

"We've got a problem!" she yelled.

The Merrow nearest the top got its second claw onto the deck and screeched. Lizzie narrowed her gaze. "I told you to shut up!" The American girl reared her leg back and booted the Merrow in the face. It toppled over backwards and took many of its ugly friends with it.

Brendan held his oar at the ready. Rory and Biddy stood on the rail with butter knives held like staffs. Sean was unconscious and lying on the deck near the cauldron.

Lizzie stood in her martial arts stance, her body as her only weapon. Dorian knew they weren't going to be enough. She looked at her own hands. The golden glow from her magic vile was zapped. She withdrew a green vile and poured it into her palms. She let it absorb for a moment, and then she closed her eyes to concentrate.

In the meantime, Brendan and Lizzie were battling the Merrows as they climbed aboard. Brendan was swinging away and knocking Merrows near and far. Lizzie kicked, punched, elbowed, kneed, jumped, flipped, and did whatever she could to hold back as many as possible. They were fighting valiantly, but it was only a matter of time before they were overtaken. Dorian was not going to let that happen.

She concentrated as a couple of Merrows approached her. Their fangs and claws were bared and they intended on causing some serious harm. One horribly scary Merrow moved in with its rippling muscles and extended claws. He swiped at her and when he made contact with her body his hand was burned off as if his wrist had been hit by a laser. He writhed in pain as the other Merrows moved in on Dorian. Each time it was the same, Merrows fell around her burned and in agony. Finally, she felt strong enough.

She pulled her limbs in tight to her body and crouched to the deck. She held this position for only a beat or two. Brendan was sweating and bleeding from multiple scratches when he happened to glance her way. When she stood up and extended her arms and legs, he could only marvel at what she was doing.

Energy or magic or whatever it was radiated from her body. Any Merrow unlucky enough to be too near Dorian was incinerated like a nuclear bomb had just been detonated. The other Merrows were burned or fled for their lives. All of the Merrows who hadn't been on the ship escaped injury but were cast at least seventy miles away from the ship.

No trace of the Merrows remained on board. Only a scorched deck where Dorian had been standing gave evidence of her brave action.

Brendan had closed his eyes once the green wave was upon him. He had thought that it was the end of him as well, but the wave passed through him harmlessly. Lizzie, Rory, and Biddy seemed no worse for wear, either. Only Sean was laid out on the deck, but even he was beginning to come to.

They gathered around Sean and helped him to a sitting position. The old timer coughed and wiped the grit off of his face. "What happened?" he asked.

Brendan shook his head in disbelief. "It was wild, Sean. Dorian did something and they all either died or got the hell out of here."

Sean looked over at Dorian. She still radiated a slight greenish glow. "How many vials do you have left?"

"Five," she said with the slightest regret in her voice.

Sean leaned on his crutch and Brendan helped him to his feet. "Well, five is better than none. Besides, if you didn't use one we wouldn't be having this conversation."

"That had to be the strangest thing that I have ever lived through," Brendan remarked.

"What about the time you went to the hospital because you had that toy car stuck up your… " Lizzie began.

"No! No!" Brendan interrupted. "This was still stranger." He shot his sister a look and she smiled. He couldn't help but feel a wave of relief wash over him and he smiled, too. It caught him totally off guard when his cell phone rang.

He answered it.

Oscar held his phone to his ear, but it was a difficult task given the state he was in. His vision was a little blurry and his head felt too large for his neck to support. He leaned against the wood-planked wall for some stabilization.

"Hey, Son," he hiccupped. "How are you kids doing?"

Brendan was pretty sure he knew what was going on with his dad since he sounded like this every New Year's Eve, but he didn't say anything about it. "Are you feeling okay, Dad?"

Oscar made a motion to shoo off any concerns by waving his hand around in the air. Brendan didn't see it. "I'm fine, fine, fine. I just wanted to call before you all went to bed."

Brendan glanced out at the sky and looked at the beginning of a sunrise and chuckled. "The sun is coming up, Dad."

It took Oscar a moment to process the words. "Huh? Sunrise? Well, anyway, these fellas in Gilshery have been telling me some pretty interesting stories about the

O'Neal bunch, so when I get a chance I'm gonna check out a little place called Corways."

Brendan covered the phone and looked over at Dorian. "Dad says he's going to go to Corways later."

"Well, if we don't get to my father on time then he may not find anyone there anyway," Dorian replied. The stress of the situation was etched on her face.

Rory stood up and stretched. "He may find a bunch of little dead bodies or crazed blood-thirsty Leprechauns." Rory thought for a moment. "Yeah, probably blood-thirsty."

"Now, that would be grand, right?" Biddy said sarcastically. "Why don't you shut that big mouth of yours?"

Brendan knitted his brow and held the phone back to his ear just in time to hear his father belch.

"Oh, excuse me, Son," chuckled his father. "Look, I got to go. We're doing one last round of singing. See you tomorrow."

Brendan disconnected the call and looked out at the serene water. He wasn't focused on the lack of mobility the ship now had. He didn't think about the fact that they appeared to be dead in the water. He was still confused by the conversation with his dad.

Dorian noticed too. "What?"

Brendan had an odd, quizzical look. "He's, ah, singing at a bar."

Dorian just shrugged. "When in Rome."

"But I thought he was in Gilshery," Rory interrupted.

Biddy held her forehead in her hand. "Just stop talking."

"What?" Rory asked.

Dorian was only half-listening to the other Leprechauns' argument. She was more focused on how to get the travel back into the travelers. "Is there anything we can do to make this thing go, Sean?"

The old captain studied the air and the sea and shook his head. "Not without a major wind, Dorian."

The air had not only left the sails, but it had left their spirits too. They were feeling deflated and frustrated. Dorian couldn't help but think about how close they were to Scotland. There wasn't much left to the journey, but they were stalled and that was killing her.

Lizzie sat on the rail and tried not to think about any of the craziness. How many times had she almost died? She was beginning to lose count. It was too many times for a fifteen year old, that was for certain. What was she thinking coming on this adventure? Some of the images she had seen to this point were going to stay with her forever. They would haunt her nightmares. The worst part was that it wasn't even over yet. They hadn't really accomplished anything. There wasn't even a breeze to make them even think that they were going to make it as far as Scotland.

About that time in her thoughts, she felt her hair begin to move. She looked around at the others, but Rory and Biddy were arguing and Dorian, Sean, and Brendan were in low conversation. None of them seemed to be feeling anything. Lizzie glanced upward and spotted the flag on the top of the mast come to life. It started as a small amount of movement, but then it began to whip around.

"Hey, guys," Lizzie spoke up. "I think our wind is here."

The others looked up just as the sails ballooned and filled with a massive gust of wind. They were all struggling to remain on their feet as the ship started sharply towards Scotland.

"Okay," shouted Sean. "With any luck we'll make it across in record time!"

Brendan laughed. "We have a bunch of Leprechauns with us; I don't think it gets any luckier than that."

The wind pushed the ship like a rock skimming the surface of a lake. The travelers were being bounced and jostled and thrown about once the ship really got going. Lizzie fell rear-end first into an open barrel. Luckily for her, it only had coils of rope on the inside. Rory and Biddy rolled right off of a table and landed unceremoniously into the dirty end of a crusty mop. Brendan was sloshed right off his feet and landed with a thud on his backside. Fortunately or unfortunately for Brendan, Dorian did the same and landed on top of him.

Brendan held her in his arms and they looked at each other, both grinning from ear to ear.

"Oh, sorry," Dorian said quickly. "I lost my balance."

"Yeah," Brendan added softly. "Me too."

She could feel herself being drawn into him. His eyes, his lips, that grin. They were all so tempting. She leaned closer following his lead.

"Whoa!" shouted Lizzie from a deck above. "Look at the sails!"

She pointed directly up the mast and everyone's eyes followed. A shimmering mass was beginning to flash into vision. They all knew instantly who it was.

"Artie!" shouted Dorian, getting to her feet. "We're so glad to see you."

"I heard the Merrows' song and I knew you lot were in trouble," said the ghost. His form was bloated as if he were a cloud.

"Well, that definitely solves the mystery of the freaky wind gust," commented Lizzie.

"Besides, you all looked so pitiful bobbing on the water that I had no choice but to come out and lend a hand." Gorgoch smiled. He felt useful again. He always felt that way when he was helping the living or fighting off the monsters of the night. Seeing how happy Dorian was really warmed his heart. He did feel a little bit ashamed of appearing, though. His plan was to get them across and drift back to Ireland, but when that American was about to kiss her, well, Artie changed his plans. "Then I figured that you could use my help in Scotland after all."

"What about Morna? Aren't you still worried about her taking control of you again?" asked Brendan.

"I think I need to take that chance," replied Artie with a little too sharp of a tone in his voice. He calmed it down immediately. "No one else knows the way. I'm your only hope of reaching the castle in time."

"Scotland off the starboard," Sean called out. "We'll be there in a few minutes, kids. Prepare yourselves."

A dark voyeur circled high above the ship. The spy, having seen enough, flew off towards Morna's castle.

Chapter 12
✝ The Black Forest ✝

DESPITE IT BEING SUNRISE, the area around Morna's castle was conspicuously void of substantial light. The perpetual darkness was spawned by her dark magic and was slowly creeping further out into Scotland. Dark magic had invaded the once lush and lively forest long before Morna's time. Residents of the nearby land could never recall a time when the forest wasn't black and cold and frightening. In fact, for six-hundred years the forest had been dark and spooky. Conchar had cast it into darkness long ago as his hatred for humans grew. Morna was only too happy to continue the trend.

Morna and Dullahan stood in silence as the griffin approached from the southeast. When the beast landed and its talons gently scraped the stone floor, Morna waited patiently for news. The griffin hesitated, so it was no surprise to her to find out that Duncan's annoyingly resilient daughter and her friends had escaped the Merrows.

"So, the Merrows have failed." She contemplated the situation before speaking again. "Fools. They weren't useful in the wars either."

The griffin screeched again and this time Morna found that she was surprised. "Gorgoch speeds them over the sea?" She clenched her fist and blood-red plasma dripped from between her fingers and dropped to the stone floor. When the plasma struck the cold tile it sizzled and evaporated. Morna was not pleased at this turn of events.

She turned to Dullahan. "There was no doubt that Gorgoch would step in to fight against you—he has always done that—but to come back home to Scotland, well, that's something entirely different." She thought again and her mind twisted and turned over with an idea. She cackled like the witches of television and the movies and shook the rest of the plasma to the floor. It sizzled as she spoke. "The fool returns to Scotland, hmmm. This little group is not to be touched until they enter the Black Forest. They will be too late by nightfall anyway, but I really want to watch these over-zealous travelers die. Let's make sure that happens, Dullahan."

He bowed and exited the tower. Morna turned back to the griffin. "Once Duncan's will is finally broken, I'll consolidate the Pure Powers of the Leprechauns, the Sidhes, and the Merrows with my own dark magic. I hope these fools survive long enough to face me." She smiled a smile that would make even the Grinch run and hide.

✦ ✦ ✦

The ship docked with little fanfare. There were only a handful of boats docked and a couple of fisherman milled around rolling nets or doing other maintenance.

Gorgoch shrunk to human size and joined the others on deck. "Once we step foot on shore we'll need to be very cautious."

Sean nodded his agreement. "Ghosty's right. The old witch has many eyes watching her lands."

"She probably knows we're here already," finished Gorgoch.

"Okay," began Dorian. "Gather your things and meet on the dock." She immediately went to the cauldron and searched around for any item she may have left behind. She checked her bag and took a mental inventory. She had five vials of magic remaining. She decided to leave the ladle, the iodine, and other useless stuff. She did, however, take a coil of rope and a small purse-full of the golden residue that remained in the bottom of the cauldron. One never knew when a magical force field could come in handy.

Lizzie hid Rory and Biddy away in her own backpack to keep them out of the sight of the fishermen. Plus she figured that they would be easier to spot as a group if tiny Leprechauns were strolling about. They walked down the ramp, and she took a seat on an old foldout chair on the small boardwalk.

Brendan didn't have anything to carry, so he started to clean up the deck. He righted the toppled boxes and chairs. He started to grab a broom, but Sean walked over to him.

"Hey, thanks for taking us over here," said Brendan.

"Glad to help," replied Sean. "These are tough times that we're living in."

"Sounds like it," agreed Brendan.

"Reminds me of when I was a young Leprechaun round about the beginning of the War of Magicks." Sean stared hard at Brendan and waited. "Tough times those were, as well."

Brendan looked back at Sean. He had to know. "Have we meet before this boat ride, Sean, because I have this feeling like I know you."

"I'm relieved to hear you say that because I think I remember from where I know you." Sean thought a moment more. "It may sound strange. I have never seen you before, but I have felt your presence."

"I'm not following you."

"Long ago, before the War, I was having a conversation

with a cousin of mine and our friend. At the time I felt a presence with us, but I didn't pay it much mind. That was until I felt your presence again when you stepped onto my ship." Sean smiled. "I knew right then that it was you."

"But how's that possible? I'm seventeen!"

"You live in a world where things don't always make sense, Brendan. I bet before a few days ago, you thought magic only existed in the movies. You were there, Brendan, and that means something."

Brendan conceded as his vision came back to him. "I had this dream before Dullahan attacked us. I went back and saw things that until now I thought I just made up in my imagination." Brendan breathed out a short breath of disbelief. "You were at the campfire. I don't know why I didn't recognize it when I saw you today."

Dorian walked over to the guys. "You ready, Brendan?"

Brendan looked over to Sean. "Thanks again."

Sean smiled an old man's smile. "Good luck to you both."

They left Sean to his boat and they joined Lizzie, Rory, and Biddy on the boardwalk. Gorgoch held his human size but drifted out of human vision. He would stay hidden until they found the edge of town, which was devoid of wakeful and watchful eyes.

Gorgoch floated twenty feet above the others near the treetops looking to the west and at a black spot on the green landscape. He frowned and blew out the equivalent of a deep breath before drifting back to the others in mid-conversation.

"I don't know," Brendan was saying. "Do you really think it was such a good idea to send away our only ride back to Ireland?"

Dorian nodded. "Sean is old, Brendan. He can't do anything else for us." Searching Brendan's eyes she saw that he was still not convinced. "You saw him. Getting us back to the surface nearly killed him."

It was his turn to search her eyes. "It's like you don't think we'll be going back to Ireland." Dorian looked away and at Gorgoch as he took on a visible form. "You don't think we're going to win, do you?"

Again, Dorian didn't reply. She wanted to say with the utmost confidence that they would win. That they would storm the castle and defeat the very powerful and insane witch, but it seemed like too big of a long shot. Avoiding the question was what she needed to do. "Let's go. My father's time grows short."

Rory and Biddy were poking their heads out of the backpack listening in on the conversation. Rory agreed. "I think it best that we finish this journey sooner than later."

"Did you have another vision?" asked Lizzie.

"No. I just feel like there's something changing inside me."

Rory did look a little peaked to Lizzie.

Dorian and Lizzie began walking while Gorgoch and Brendan hung back a second. Gorgoch leaned in and said, "I fear that the longer Morna has Dorian's father in her possession, the more our Leprechaun friends are going to change."

"What do you mean?" asked Brendan.

Gorgoch cocked his head. "Think of the Sidhes and the Merrows. Neither of them have ever looked or acted that way before."

Recognition crossed Brendan's face. "You don't think Morna will actually be able to control them or something, do you?"

"I think it's not only controlling them, but changing everything about them." Gorgoch held Brendan's stare a moment longer before vanishing from sight.

Brendan only stood for a second before walking to catch up to the group. He knew now that their window of opportunity was shrinking by the second.

✦ ✦ ✦

Strange dreams played in Oscar's mind. He had weird visions of floating and soaring high above the British Isles. He saw himself soar all the way to Wales, to the coast of Glamorganshire, and into a modest hut that he normally wouldn't have even noticed. He landed on the dirt floor, and his bare toes pushed deeply into the soft ground. The place was empty and cobwebs clung heavily to all of the furniture in the place.

Oscar fumbled with the Knot Charm that he had forgotten was in his palm. The gold became so warm that he had to drop it. Dreams are funny, though, because the charm hovered in mid-air before zooming across the room and settling on an ornate music box that somehow escaped Oscar's notice. The charm sat fixed on the little box, and a strange, black florescence flared for the briefest of moments. Oscar approached with caution and gingerly extended his fingers to retrieve his charm. He was relieved when he found the charm had cooled off, but a little distraught when he found that it was securely fastened to the box.

He tugged and pulled and tried to pry the charm free, but nothing was working. He lifted the box to examine it for a solution when he blinked and found that he was flying once more on a course back to Ireland. The box was still in his hand, but at the moment he didn't seem to remember that the charm and the box were separate things. In Oscar's mind, the charm and the box became one and the same.

✦ ✦ ✦

"So, this is the Black Forest," commented Brendan as they approached.

The Black Forest was extremely sinister in looks and in feel. It was dark, of course, but it was an unnatural darkness. Brendan was very struck by the contrast of a beautiful morning sun that shone all around them and the dense darkness that enveloped the woods that they were about to enter.

"What was your first clue, Sherlock?" joked Lizzie. No one else was smiling.

Gorgoch floated to the front of the group and took to a visual form. His features were still hard to focus on since they were elusive, but he had the others' attention. "This forest is the most evil place that I have ever had the displeasure of venturing into. There are vile creatures that would sooner devour your flesh than look at you. The trees themselves plot against you. Do not think for a moment that Morna has any other desire than to see you destroyed."

"She's already tried to destroy us, Artie." Lizzie's eyes were large with fear. This was all so crazy! They had nearly been torn to bits by fairies, eaten by mermaids, and met with a fate fitting for Icabod Crane. Wasn't Gorgoch just pointing out the obvious?

Brendan knew where her mind was in all this because he wasn't far off, but he got the gist of the warning. "I think he means that it's going to get much worse, Liz."

Rory's mouth fell open. "How could it get worse?"

Gorgoch's face moved into what could only be perceived as a smile. "You haven't faced anything yet, my friends. Let's hope we can get to Duncan without having to face the witch herself."

When silence had fallen on the group, Gorgoch, remaining in mostly solid form, led them into the Black Forest.

Perched on Lizzie's backpack, Biddy whispered to Rory. "Are you afraid?"

Rory wanted to appear strong and brave. "Of course not."

Gorgoch didn't miss a beat and said, "You should be."

✦ ✦ ✦

Dullahan watched the small group enter the Black Forest. The fools were ripe for the pickings, but he would wait until he had a true tactical advantage. Attacking now, he would perhaps kill one or two of them, but the spirit would thwart his attempt to eradicate the entire group. Besides that, Morna would be none too pleased with him if they did not at least reach deep into her lands. The headless demon assumed that she wanted the group to reach her, but not before nightfall. That was key. His only real job was to slow them down, and he had a plan in mind.

✦ ✦ ✦

Upon entering the Black Forest Brendan had a few things pop into his head. Words like *spooky, scary, frightening, chilly, disheartening,* and *reparative* (the last sticking in his head since the seventh grade spelling bee). But the word that spoke volumes to him at that moment was *Zoinks*! Shaggy and Scooby had made it famous, but it never meant more to him then being in the place the ghost called, "the most evil place on Earth."

The one thing Brendan was thankful for was the fact that Gorgoch had come along. The guy was powerful and fast. He could protect them in the event of a monster attack. Besides all that, the guy sort of glowed. It wasn't obscene or overwhelming, but soft and gentle. It was comforting, really. Who would have thought that could be said about a ghost?

Lizzie and Dorian were walking shoulder to shoulder with Gorgoch in the lead. Rory and Biddy were keeping a watchful eye from the safe cover of Lizzie's backpack, which meant that Brendan was guarding the rear. He decided early on that it was a paranoid person's worst nightmare. Every time a branch would shift or a sound would call, the others would jump or gasp and that made the startling source even worse. It was beginning to feel very much like a horror movie.

Brendan did notice that they were walking a worn path where trees had been cleared away.

"This path has been here for over six-hundred years," Gorgoch said, perhaps sensing the unspoken questions the living might have. "The previous owner of the forest, Conchar, burned a path by breathing fire and decaying the trees and greenery."

"He could exhale fire?" asked Lizzie.

"He could, but the fire didn't burn," answered Gorgoch. "Conchar was so evil that his fire acted like disease and killed on command."

"Where is this Conchar now?" inquired Rory.

"No one can say for certain. He may be long dead, but I doubt it."

"Why is that?" Biddy wondered.

"I'm sure you've heard it before, but evil is hard to kill." Gorgoch turned back to look at the others. "I only tell you about the path because of its purpose. Conchar, and now Morna used it to both travel and to have human slaves transported to the castle."

"That's terrible," Dorian said with a sad shake of her head.

"It is terrible, because once the witch has the humans she mutates them." Concerned looks met his serious, ever-flowing features. "And the only way to free them is to kill them."

Silence was upon the group as they considered Gorgoch's implication. Brendan was trying to muster up the courage to tell Gorgoch that he wasn't sure that he could kill another person under any circumstances. Killing monsters and rogue fairies was one thing, but a person? Well, that was something entirely different.

A howl in the distance sparked everyone back to the present.

"Uh, what was that?" Lizzie asked in a shaky tone.

Gorgoch looked into the distance and sighed. "I fear the Cu Sith is near."

"Cu Sith?" asked Lizzie.

"I think I saw him in Star Wars," joked Rory. Biddy punched him hard in the arm.

"The Cu Sith is like a ghost dog," explained Gorgoch.

"Oh," replied Lizzie. "A nice, cute, little ghosty pup, huh?" she asked hopefully.

"More like a large predator of the soul," responded the half-spirit. "When the Cu Sith does come, avoid its touch at all costs, lest your soul be torn asunder."

"Say that again?" Lizzie said, wincing.

"Don't let the dog touch you, deary," answered Biddy.

"Great," Brendan huffed sarcastically. "Now there's a ghost dog that can rip your soul apart. Where do these freaking things come from?"

"It doesn't matter, Brendan," said Dorian with hard-set eyes. "I'm going to help protect you."

"Protect me? I don't need you to... how are you going

to do that?" Brendan asked.

Dorian reached into her bag and removed the five vials that she had remaining. She held them out in her palm for the others to see. "Each of you needs to select a vial and pour the contents into your palms."

Brendan reached out and selected the silver vial. Lizzie took the purple while Rory got the blue and Biddy the orange. That left Dorian with the red which she instantly poured into her hands. Her hands began to glow red and a split second later the glow spread over the rest of her body as well. They looked at each other in anticipation and then followed Dorian's lead and poured the magic into their palms.

Rory's hands began to glow and then the glow manifested itself as a bow and a quiver of arrows. "Wow! That's cool!" said Rory.

"Just don't shoot any of us, alright?" joked Brendan. Rory gave a nod of agreement and smiled.

Biddy's back sprouted wings of orange. She started to float without trying. "Whoa! I'm flying here!"

"Way to go, Biddy," laughed Lizzie.

Brendan's silver glow shot down his right arm and extended out into the shape of a sword. When the magic had finished, he held the sword and marveled at its craftsmanship. "Now that's crazy."

Lizzie was all smiles as her magical purple glow hummed and moved to her right hand as well. "Come on sword… or wings… or something awesome," she wished. Her magic extended out further and further until it showed itself.

"I get a stick!" cursed Lizzie. "A stinking stick?"

Gorgoch smiled briefly and looked down the path. "I feel that we must hurry." Gorgoch, Dorian, and Brendan started ahead of Lizzie, Rory, and Biddy.

Rory patted Lizzie on the shoulder. "Sticks are cool."

"Yeah," agreed Biddy from the air next to Lizzie's head. "They're really cool."

The threesome started to follow, but Lizzie just stared at her stick.

"Man, this sucks." She moped after her group with her staff in hand.

Chapter 13

✛ Courage ✛

GROANS, MOANS, and the low rattles of breathing were the only things Duncan could hear in his cage. The sad part was that he wasn't aware if he was making the noises or if his cellmates were. He could see that Osis was floating near the top of her cage like a kid doing the Dead Man's Float with her friends in the pool, only he wasn't sure if she wasn't dead. He wanted to ask, but that was going to take energy and that was something that he just didn't have enough to expend for the question. He was concentrating on keeping Morna out of his mind, out of his magic, and that was draining all of his energies.

Duncan spared a look in Wardicon's direction, and his old friend was curled up like a ball; his chest was slowly rising and falling. The Sidhe King's will power was long gone, and his mind, body, and clan were now under the control of the witch.

That's what she wanted. She was after the magic, but Duncan knew that she was also building an army. But why? What need did she have for an army? She also seemed to want to add the Leprechauns to that disdainful hoard. He was not about to let her have them.

Not while he was king.

✦ ✦ ✦

The travelers walked cautiously along the path. All, except Lizzie, of course, were thrilled with their new magical weapons, but none of them were really looking forward to using them. If it came time for them to put the weapons to the test, then that meant they were under attack. They all knew it would happen, but that didn't mean that they had to look forward to it.

Gorgoch stopped the group when they entered a diminutive clearing. There was a small river that was roiling ahead of them with much faster moving water than what would have been expected considering that it was a small river and the terrain was relatively level. It hadn't rained much, as far as Brendan could recall, so it just looked weird.

"That's one fast-moving river," stated Rory.

"That's what I was thinking," agreed Brendan.

"Don't forget that it flows through a cursed forest," pointed out Dorian. "It's not like it has to follow the normal rules of nature."

"Good point." It unnerved Brendan to think about magic as a real thing. He was only just beginning to understand the world, and now his experiences in Ireland and Scotland were teaching him something entirely different. He wondered what Newton would have thought about all this.

The group walked further on the path and spotted a creaky wooden bridge. "That's where we'll have to cross," said Gorgoch lifting one ghostly hand to gesture toward the bridge.

"You think?" scoffed Lizzie sarcastically.

"Keep your eyes open, folks. This is a good place for an ambush," Dorian said readying her hands. They began to glow red and emitted a crackling energy.

They drew closer to the bridge and had a much better view of the river. It was bubbling and foaming and flowing like mad. It was also black. It didn't look like oil or sludge, but like regular river water, only dark and opaque.

"Okay," began Brendan. "Is that the grossest water ever or what?"

"It's pretty gross," agreed Lizzie.

Gorgoch searched the area suspiciously. "I have a bad

feeling."

Just as he finished his sentence a streak of green shot out of the trees and slammed into Gorgoch smashing him to the ground. The green form and Gorgoch slid through trees even though the trees tried to move, they were too slow and became shattered into a million shards. The pair were instantly out of sight.

"Gorgoch!" called Dorian. Whatever had attacked him had dragged him away.

"What in the world was that?" asked Lizzie.

"I believe that was the Cu Sith," answered Biddy. "Let's hope it can't take Gorgoch's soul."

"Isn't he all soul?" asked Brendan.

"Oh, bad dog!" called Lizzie. "You leave him alone."

A moment later the river itself came to life and spewed forth several boiling forms onto the shore. They seethed and roiled on the spot changing into different shapes, all of them menacing and gruesome.

"What in the world are those ugly things?" asked Lizzie.

"Those are Kelpies," answered Rory. "They are fowl creatures."

The Kelpies shape-shifted into hideous monsters. One became a dragon while another became a minotaur. Two others resembled velociraptors. The rest took the form of demons. Though they all came in different forms, none of them could shake the black water look. They all boiled and bubbled and roiled within the shell of the creatures they became.

"What are we supposed to do against these things?" Rory said with a cracking voice.

"We take them out and we do it fast." Dorian took the lead and the five squared off against the black water Kelpies.

The Kelpies hissed and bared their fangs. The dragon let out a battle cry and the Kelpies sprang into action. Dorian didn't have to tell the others to fight because the fight was brought to them.

The odds were overwhelming at seven to one, but the five had magic on their side. Sure, they were fighting hideous creatures of the dark with killer claws and stupendous strength. The group didn't have the numbers on their side or the home-field advantage. All of that didn't seem to make that big of a difference though, since each one of them had become supercharged by Dorian's gifts.

Demons charged at Rory who was perched atop a stone on the banks. He let loose with an arrow and nailed an ugly Kelpie between the eyes. It fell to the banks in a splash. Rory was ready to reach back to find another arrow, but one appeared in his bow without his help.

"Now that is cool," he exclaimed. He continued to fire at the Kelpies. He had a moment and looked out to find Biddy. She was in the air avoiding the slashing claws of a few of the demon Kelpies.

"Keep your hands to yourselves, boys," she cried. Biddy zoomed in and out, feeling that there was nothing much she could do but cause a distraction. If that was all she could do, then she was going to do it well. She zipped around the battlefield and acted like an annoying bug.

She flew high above and tried to find a place she could be of some use. Noticing Rory was starting to bite off more than he could chew, she dove at a group of newly transforming Kelpies. "Leave him alone!"

They spotted her coming and they changed their forms into ravens and clawed at her as she drew near. She changed courses and narrowly avoided the razor sharp talons. The Kelpie ravens pursued her, and Biddy had to will herself to fly faster and harder. She could hear their hissing and feel their breath at her rear. She figured that this was it. She wasn't scared, though. She didn't give up or give in to the beasts. She turned and lashed out with her will. To her surprise, several feathers were flung from her wings and shredded the Kelpie ravens to pieces. Black water splashed against her face as the creatures rained down on the earth below.

Dorian looked up as droplets of black rain fell from the sky. The drops sizzled away as they neared her and her magical red glow. She looked out at the river and watched as more Kelpies rose and transformed into one creature or another. She blasted here and there and evaporated many of the filthy beasts. She mostly watched out for her friends as she kept one eye on the large dragon that squatted on the bridge and hissed and roared.

Brendan decided that he was going to be fearless. What reason was there not to be? The creatures were made of water, after all. How tough and scary could that be?

He soon found out.

The smaller demon-like Kelpies weren't much trouble, but when the Minotaur charged, Brendan was put on the defensive. This Kelpie was huge and fast. It exhaled a black mist as it ran at Brendan. The American dodged to the right and rolled to his feet in time to see the Minotaur annihilate a very large and thick oak. Now he knew why he should have been somewhat frightened.

The giant, ugly creature didn't bother to turn around to face him again. Instead it reformed itself, and the face poked out of the back of its head. It let out a fear-inducing battle cry and charged again.

"Whoa!" Brendan exclaimed as he spun away and slashed at the creature's leg. The blade passed through with little resistance, but the creature showed no effect. He could see it smile as it turned back again. It held out its arm and a giant club took the place of its hand.

"Come on! That's not even fair," Brendan admonished.

The beast slammed his club down and nearly crushed Brendan. A quick step to the left allowed him to keep breathing. It lashed out again with the heavy club and drove Brendan back. It slammed the club down and Brendan backed away. The scene played out like that until Brendan teetered on the bank of the black river.

The Minotaur paused and looked at Brendan as if to say that the end was near. Brendan glanced down at the babbling blackness and he knew that if he went in there then it was the end.

"Can't we talk about this?" asked Brendan.

The Minotaur shook its head slowly.

Brendan narrowed his eyes and stared at the creature defiantly. "Okay, chump, bring it."

The large Kelpie reared back with its club and then dropped it down at Brendan with tremendous intentions to crush. Brendan raised his sword to block and when the two connected, something incredible happened. Brendan lost his footing and nearly fell into the water. The only thing that kept him out of it was the fact that his sword was stuck in the Minotaur's club.

The beast hissed and laughed until it realized that Brendan hadn't fallen into the water. It looked around for him and then spotted him dangling from the club.

Brendan looked sweepingly back at the ugly thing and waved. "Hi. Uh, don't mind me."

The beast grew furious and tried to shake him loose. Brendan called out for help.

Lizzie held her stick out and cursed silently at her bad magical luck. "Stupid stick," she mumbled.

The demon Kelpies didn't care that she was unhappy with her weapon and didn't bother to wait for her to get a new one before they attacked. If they would have been smart they would have waited, or better yet, they would have ran.

They charged her with the insane rage of hungry predators, but when she began to splatter the Kelpies in every direction with her staff, they started to take a new approach. They circled around her, and they looked like they felt confident.

Lizzie saw their plan. "That's a bad move, fellas."

They charged all at once, but Lizzie was too fast for them. She leapt into the air and spun. She forced her staff out in a wide circle and by the time she had landed her attackers had been reduced to puddles of black water.

"Lizzie," hollered Dorian. "How are you holding up?"

Lizzie looked at the black carnage and smiled, "Oh, I'm good."

She turned her head when a cry for help rang out from the banks of the river. "Brendan!" She ran as fast as she could to help.

"There's no way that I'm going into that water, pal!" Brendan clung to his sword for dear life as the beast unsuccessfully tried to shake him loose.

Suddenly, the creature stopped shaking Brendan and held a very surprised look on its face.

"What the … ?" said Brendan in surprise.

The beast dropped to its knees and Brendan's feet found soft footing on the grass. He yanked his sword free and glanced down where a purple staff was jammed up in between the Minotaur's legs. Brendan looked past the beast's big head and saw Lizzie waving from just behind its shoulder.

"Oh, thanks, Liz," he said.

He slashed out and chopped the Minotaur's head off with a single motion. The head and body held their form until they landed in the black water. There were absorbed by the current.

"Nice use of stick, little sister," smiled Brendan.

"You know, sticks are cool," she smiled back.

They ran back into the battle to help Dorian with the Dragon.

✦ ✦ ✦

Dullahan was enjoying the show from his vantage point astride his demon steed. The horse was anxious to charge down the path and enter into battle as well, but Dullahan held the reigns steady. The stallion only tugged a few times before it got the message. It took to snorting out balls of fire and making the trees shift their roots to avoid the heat.

Dullahan didn't mind or care about the trees at that moment. He was too busy making notes about his adversaries. They fought well with their Leprechaun weapons. The small Leprechauns were moderately effective while the Leprechaun princess showed that she was a good leader and a valiant warrior. The humans were holding their own as well. The Kelpies hardly stood a chance, but Dullahan knew that before he sent the mindless fools into battle. The group was much more formidable since he had first faced them on the road in Ireland. They had courage and skill and of course they had that insipid Gorgoch, but they were also short on time. That desperation was going to be their undoing. That was going to make them take chances, and that gave him the advantage.

✦ ✦ ✦

Gorgoch was having a hard time dealing with the vicious jaws of the Cu Sith. It had already shone that it could tear through his visceral being. Luckily for him the ghost dog only tore at the vapor-like clothing that he wore, but that was enough to make Gorgoch know that this apparition could do him some serious harm.

The jaws snapped shut in blood-thirsty bites attempting to separate Gorgoch's spirit half from this realm. Gorgoch had his forearm in the Cu Sith's throat, so that prevented it from laying its large fangs into his ghostly form.

"Heel!" he commanded.

The beast had all the leverage, though, while it had him pinned on his back. Normally he would just turn to vapor and move away from the threat, but the Cu Sith could do the same thing, and then it might take him out while they were in that form. He was stuck for a moment unless something in this dynamic changed.

When Brendan and Lizzie arrived at Dorian's side, they saw a young woman who was powerful, smart, and agile. They also saw a Kelpie dragon that was all of those things but also enormous. They were all nearly vaporized by the dragon's version of fire breath. Dodging to the right, Brendan caught a whiff of the toxic fumes the thing spewed down at them and he nearly puked.

"Oh man!" exclaimed Lizzie. "That has to smell worse than your soccer shoes."

Normally, Brendan would have responded in kind, but the dragon lashed out with its large claw and nearly smashed him. Jibbing his sister took a place on the back burner.

Dorian launched three consecutive blasts into the beast's throat, but the thing showed little effect. It absorbed the attacks and gave it back to them in return. It slashed claws, snapped its jaws, whipped its tail, and spit stench-fire. The three were nimble, but growing weary from the battle. A tail caught Brendan and knocked him headlong into one of the bridge posts. The backside of the creature's paw connected with Lizzie and threw her some twenty feet away. That left Dorian.

"Fine, you foul bugger," Dorian railed in anger. "You are going to wish that you never tangled with a Leprechaun."

The dragon roared and reared back on its hind legs. It opened its maw and launched itself at her. In a single snap it took the Leprechaun princess into its mouth.

"Nooooooooo!" screamed Brendan. He spun to his feet and charged forward with his silver sword gleaming.

The dragon snorted and shook its head. Smoke began to trail out of the side of its mouth and nostrils. Its lips parted and a red light leaked from the opening. The dragon began to wail in pain until its head finally exploded!

Dorian flipped out of the opening and landed gracefully on her feet right in front of Brendan who skidded to a stop.

"I hate Kelpies," she quipped.

They had time for exactly one smile, two chuckles, and three breaths before the entire Black River began to come to life. Hundreds of Kelpies began to emerge from the river.

Lizzie walked up behind Brendan and Dorian. "Don't

these things ever stop?"

"They are mindless creatures that can rearrange their bodies so that they never get tired. They never give up." Dorian exhaled the last of her three breaths. "It's likely that they will just wear us down and overrun us."

Biddy carried Rory over and they dropped down to land on Lizzie's shoulders. "We can take them on, Dorian," said Biddy.

"Don't give up hope yet," added Rory. "We'll get to Duncan in time."

"He's right, you know," boomed a voice from above.

The five looked up and saw the enlarged form of Gorgoch holding the Cu Sith by the scruff of its neck like a puppy.

"Aww, demon puppy," said Lizzie.

Gorgoch flung the Cu Sith way out of the Black Forest and well out of sight. His face still shimmered, but the others knew he was smiling.

"Look!" yelled Rory. "The Kelpies are running for it!"

They watched the Black River fill itself back in as the riverbed became full once more. In a matter of seconds the water was calm and slowly moving along.

Gorgoch shrank back down. "Let's go. We've been delayed too long."

With that they crossed the bridge very wary of what could be coming their way.

Chapter 14

✢ Visions from a Ghost ✢

I'M SURE THAT MORNA'S not done yet," Dorian said warningly, as if anyone present thought that she was.

Biddy's wings fluttered softly as she flew next to Lizzie's shoulder and Rory who was perched upon it. "That was some mighty fine bow work, Rory."

"Thanks, Bid," replied the small Leprechaun happily.

"And your flying was divine." Biddy blushed and waved him off before he turned to Lizzie. "Nice use of stick, Liz."

"Thanks. I guess I was a little quick to judge the weapon I was given."

Dorian chuckled a little. "From the way my father tells it, we form the weapons we wield."

"What?" Lizzie scoffed. "I mean I was pretty good back there, but there is no way I would have chosen a staff."

"Aye, but you ended up with one anyway, so that tells me that it's the weapon that would suit you best," replied Dorian.

Lizzie considered the notion while Biddy glanced over at her wings. "I just hope the magic holds up until we're done with this whole mess."

Brendan watched the conversation and noticed the way the Leprechauns were looking. It was like a fever was coming on and they were fending it off with Vitamin C, but it would eventually hit them hard enough they they wouldn't be able to fight back. Gorgoch must have seen the concern on his face.

"They are worsening," the spirit man said leaning in close to Brendan's ear. "If we take too much longer, then I fear they will no longer be under their own control."

Brendan's mind ran through all of the worst possible outcomes as they walked along the path in the Black Forest. The Black River and the bridge were behind them now and dark shadows and ominous, unforeseen dangers awaited them. The thought of the unknown was hard on Brendan. What would happen to Dorian, Rory, or Biddy if this strange illness, if it could be called that, overtook them? Would they end up like the Sidhes or the Merrows? Would it be worse than being controlled by Morna? Would they die?

After mulling around those disturbing thoughts for a while, Brendan started to focus on what would happen to him and to Lizzie. Without the help of the others how did they hope to complete the task? Gorgoch had already told them about the human slaves Morna had, and that was not a fate that Brendan wanted. A zombie-like monster at the will of a crazy old witch… no thanks. The locals called them Ruas for their glowing red eyes, a trademark of the poor devils. Not a fate that anyone would want to suffer.

They walked along in silence, listening intently to their surroundings. Any noise that was out of place, albeit in a cursed forest, drew their attention and made them ready their guard.

Brendan was getting tired of the on-edge feeling, so he decided to probe Gorgoch's memory. "Are we there yet?"

"Not quite," the ghost replied. "More obstacles await us."

"Great. Like what?" inquired Lizzie. She had calmed herself considerably after the fight with the Kelpies, but the anticipation of the next foe was making her antsy.

Gorgoch tried to think back to when he was alive and stormed the gates as a vengeful youth. Losing his love had driven him to the edge of murder, only it wasn't Dullahan or Morna that received his wrath, but the unsuspecting people that Morna had unleashed him upon. It was hard to remember anything but the hate he felt at the time. It was blind rage he supposed.

"Well, it's hard to remember."

"What do you mean?" asked Dorian.

"I came through here so fast and fueled by so much hate that I'm having a hard time remembering anything other than that." Gorgoch moved along in thought and a few memories floated to the surface of his consciousness.

"After the bridge there was… " he fought hard to pull the memory up. "Darkness."

"Well that's helpful," derided Brendan.

Three more steps showed Brendan, Lizzie, Rory, and Dorian what Gorgoch had meant. The path had led them directly over a hole in the ground that was covered in overgrowth. Gravity won out and they plummeted into the unknown darkness with a scream.

Biddy flapped her wings and looked over at Gorgoch with great surprise. He shrugged. "Oh yeah, a cave."

Biddy and Gorgoch floated down the entrance of the cave in time to see the rest of the group untangling themselves from one another. Lucky for Rory, he was laid out flat on top of the pile.

"Crickey!" the little man cried. "A little warning would have been nice there."

"Sorry about that," replied Gorgoch with a shimmering smile. "I forgot what the darkness was." Gorgoch made his visceral self glow a bit brighter and shed a modicum of light in the small room.

Brendan got to his feet first and offered his hands to

Lizzie and Dorian. He pulled them up and they all glanced around the cavern.

"Wow, it's cozy in here," Brendan joked as he felt the dampness on his backside and tried in vain to wipe it off. He held his sword aloft and pointed it back up the entrance. The sword illuminated the smooth, steeply-pitched slide that they just tobogganed down. "Good thing it wasn't just a straight fall."

"That's for sure," agreed Biddy. "It was probably fifteen meters or so."

"That would have left a mark," chuckled Rory. Halfway through his laugh a fit of coughs set in and made him struggle to breathe.

Brendan looked around the small cavern and took note of the few cave characteristics that he learned about in Earth Science. There were small stalagmites and stalactites that littered the ceiling and the floor. The walls glistened with small flecks of crystals that formed as water ran down carving out the cave over thousands of years. The cave opened up to a thin passage that was a dozen meters opposite the entrance. The floor's gradient sloped in a subtle manner.

"Well, Gorgoch, do we go to the passage or back topside?"

Gorgoch thought back and he sighed. "We have to move forward, but I want to warn you that down these passages was where I was snatched up and taken to Morna."

"I think the warning of danger goes without saying,"

offered Dorian. "Let's go."

It was eerie, really, being back in the same place where life had essentially ended. Gorgoch was young and strong then. He was alive, at least physically. Emotionally, well, that was another story. He tried to not relive the last day of his life, but memories have a funny way of being seen, especially when they aren't wanted.

Brendan walked in the lead of the pack beside the ghost man. Dorian brought up the rear with Lizzie carrying Rory on her shoulder and Biddy gliding beside her in the middle.

The cave was nothing special, as far as Brendan could tell—it was just dark. The glow of all things magical that they brought along shed enough light that finding sure footing and a walkable path wasn't really difficult. He wasn't at all concerned about the cave itself. What was concerning him were the flashes of a vision that kept poking into his mind and into his line of sight.

The vision was scary. A young man with a lantern was limping ahead of them on the path. He had dark brown hair down to his shoulders and looked like he was straight out of the seventeen hundreds. He was sweating and breathing heavily and his leg had been damaged somewhere along the way.

Brendan looked at the others, but they gave no indication that they saw the guy. Gorgoch may have seen the vision, but who could tell with his elusive facial features.

Brendan looked back to the young man in his vision

and watched.

✦ ✦ ✦

How old was he when he died? Twenty-three? Twenty-six? It was hard to remember. It didn't matter, really. The circumstances mattered and they stayed with a person well beyond the body and this world.

It was hot that night. He had charged into the Black Forest, probably the only one to do so to that point, with revenge on his heart. That witch had taken every thing from him… He was angry. Hate made his body feel that much hotter. The steamy night didn't help things.

The forest was empty except for the trees that seemed to move and slide, changing the path, changing his course. They lead him over the Black River and into the cave. Why hadn't he remembered that? Memories are funny.

He fell and slid all the way down like the others did, only his leg slammed into a rock that jutted from the ground. He had smashed through it, but it reeked havoc on his knee. He was sure he had heard something snap. His lantern had skidded away from him and settled itself after tracing circles on the stone floor. He should have just laid there and cooled off. He probably could have crawled back up, but he wasn't there to let his beloved's murder go without revenge. He crawled over to the lantern and then got to his feet. He spotted the long passageway and limped towards it. They were going to pay, the witch and her demon.

The young man half dragged his left leg as he paused to look at a puddle of reflecting water. It had a weird effect. It appeared to go fifty or sixty feet deep, but the boy accidentally kicked a stone into it and it only sunk a few inches before it came to rest. The boy laughed a hearty "Ha!" and then limped ahead. Brendan looked down at the stone as he and the others followed the boy.

The path ahead opened up and the guy limped on unaware of the many dark shadows that moved on the walls and ceiling.

He should have seen them coming. Why hadn't he just looked up or at the walls or even in the reflection of the water? Gorgoch knew the answer. He was blinded and foolish. Fools usually died.

✦ ✦ ✦

Were the shadows a vision or were they happening at that moment as they were traveling? Brendan glanced around nervously.

"Does anyone see anything?"

They all responded with a "no" or "not yet," but Brendan remained alert. Alert enough for a guy having a vision, at least.

✦ ✦ ✦

They crawled on the walls like they were spiders. It was unnatural for creatures that large to cling to stone that way. Gorgoch wanted to admonish himself for not seeing the slaves, but how could he. He hadn't known they were there. He had no idea that they even existed! He was a fool, but it was more out of ignorance than a stubborn refusal to acknowledge a truth. The latter was much worse. Either way it didn't help him now.

✦ ✦ ✦

The first thing that came at the boy was hideous and frightening. It was male and had corded, rippling muscles and long, stringy, wet hair. Its red eyes glowed in the lantern's light and its gaping maw snapped open and shut.

The boy only had time to jump backwards and narrowly miss being the thing's feast. It hissed and growled like a predator. It slashed out with its hands and nails attempting to tear through the boy. Again the boy moved. Brendan was surprised how agile the boy was with his gimpy leg, but adrenaline must have been coursing through his veins.

The boy reached behind his back and quickly unveiled a flintlock musket. It must have been preloaded because he blasted the thing attacking him and drove it back ten feet or so. The musket was so loud and bright that Brendan thought there was no way that the others didn't see and hear it, too. He looked back, but again they gave no signs of noticing anything.

The red-eyed monster rolled down the embankment and settled in the small pool. The gunpowder wafted through the stale air and Brendan crinkled his nose. The few moments must have been terrifying for the boy. The Ruas leapt from the walls and ceiling and surrounded him. To his credit the young man snarled his lip and held the musket like a baseball bat. He walloped the things as they attacked, but soon the numbers became too much.

✦ ✦ ✦

"How many of them had there been?" mused Gorgoch.

He was easily outnumbered but he was strong and young and cocky. He swung that gun and smashed in heads, but the beasts were also strong and they were filled with evil and drive. They weren't going to stop. They were Morna's slaves; her walking dead. He shivered, still feeling their corpsy fingers close on his flesh. He cried out and then the memory faded.

✦ ✦ ✦

The creatures tore at the boy's clothes and slammed their fists into his body and head. The boy yelled and fought back, but it didn't take long for him to fall into unconsciousness. Brendan tried to avert his eyes because the beasts were threatening to pull the young man's limbs off his body, but the vision wouldn't allow him to look away. It was important somehow for him to see, to understand.

A large Rua lifted the boy by his throat with one hand and opened its ugly mouth that was filled with sharp black teeth. It was like the guy's head was an apple and this creature was in the mood for a snack. Its mouth opened wider than any human's mouth was capable of and pulled the boy's head in close. Just before the bite, though, a commanding voice from deep within the caves shouted for the creature to stop.

The red-eye hesitated and then continued to pull the boy's head into its maw. Something spun through the air cutting a current as it gleamed in the already dim light. Seconds later the large Rua's head fell away from its shoulders as the boy's unconscious form crumpled to the stone floor. A familiar figure marched out of the shadows and plucked a hatchet from the clavicle of the decapitated red-eye.

Dullahan wiped the ax head on the thing's chest and slid the weapon back into its loop.

"Bring the boy," he echoed to the other red-eyes.

Two thin Ruas knelt down and picked up the boy by the armpits. They trailed behind Dullahan as he exited the cave. The many other red-eyes began to devour the dead one's body in the meantime. Waste not, want not.

Chapter 15
✦ The Witch's Ruas ✦

THE VISION FADED and Brendan was left with the darkened cave. What a crazy thing to see! Images that no person would want to see! Why did he have to see it? What did it mean?

"I think we need to be cautious in this part of the cave," he said.

"What are you talking about?" asked Rory. "There's nothing here but a little pool."

"No," Gorgoch spoke up. "He's right. This place is cursed with evil."

Dorian nodded and allowed her eyes to roam the dimly lit cavern. Nothing seemed out of place, yet their was something in the air. Something that gave her chills.

The group walked cautiously on the thin path, and both Gorgoch and Brendan's eyes scanned the shadows on the walls and ceilings.

"What are you looking for?" Gorgoch asked the young American.

"Ruas," answered Brendan.

Gorgoch shook his head knowingly. That's why the memories had flooded him in this place. Brendan was some sort of clairvoyant, a vision catcher. Gorgoch should have seen it before. He wasn't sure if he had just piggybacked off of the boy's sight or vice versa.

Brendan scanned the walls, and then he saw them. Red orbs flared to life on the far right. Then another set of eyes popped up on the left. Next thing they knew the room was lit up like Christmas lights with a hundred pair of eyes flaring from every shadow of the cavern.

"Looks like they didn't want to disappoint you," said Gorgoch.

Brendan hardened his features and whipped his sword around in preparation. "Who were they again?"

Gorgoch shrugged. "They were the poor locals who have been enslaved by the witch."

"Are they alive?" asked Lizzie. The last thing she wanted to do was hurt real people. It was one thing to smash a stick into a Kelpie's face but to bash a human was quite another.

"In a way," answered the spirit man. "But don't be fooled into thinking that you can bring them back to the human world. The human side is dead."

"Think of them as shells, Lizzie," added Dorian. "You're going to have to crack those shells, hon."

The slaves could be heard growling and shuffling along the walls and ceiling apparently surrounding the travelers. The group readied themselves with their backs to the center. Each held their magical weapon with a purpose.

The Ruas slowly came into view and Brendan breathed out a slow breathe of preparation. He held the sword out like a knight. "Be ready, guys. Here they come."

✦ ✦ ✦

Dullahan stood well off in the shadow in the cave's opening to watch. If he'd had a head he would have smiled. The Leprechauns, the humans, and the meddlesome Gorgoch were about to be in big trouble. If the mindless, savage slaves could just delay the little rescue party for enough time, then the Leprechauns would be out of the equation and the humans would join the throng of slaves. Dullahan was hoping for an entertaining show, no matter how it turned out.

✦ ✦ ✦

Duncan was vaguely aware that his cage was in motion. The grunts of a guard and the creaking of one the wheels was the only noise he recognized. Sometime after the cage started moving it stopped. He heard the wind from somewhere off to the right and the scraping of some long talons on a stone floor. He thought that the griffin was clawing at the ground so that meant that he was in the tower. A large cold wave swept into the room, and it wasn't the wind.

The air felt heavy and pressed in on him. He was feeling terrible as it was, but resisting Morna with her being that close in proximity was difficult and growing more difficult with every second that passed.

"How are we feeling today, Duncan?" cackled the witch.

Duncan's willpower was dwindling and he sensed the witch's magic forcing its way into his. Its tendrils were slippery and crafty. He had been holding her assaults at bay, but how could he expect to continue?

"Give in," Morna prodded. "You've been so brave, little one. No one would blame you."

Her voice was like a memory or a dream. It floated into his head and played with his will. He half thought that it was his voice trying to convince him to stop the resistance. It would be so much easier to just give in.

"Don't worry, Duncan. You will be able to rest soon. I've almost got you." A wicked smiled played at her lips as the delicious thought of all that power was so temptingly close to her grasp.

✦ ✦ ✦

The Rua hoard attacked like a mob storming a wall with

sharp, jagged nails, powerful bodies, and hungry jaws. They were fast and that surprised Lizzie. In the movies they usually made them out to be plodding and sloth-like, but these suckers were like ninjas and pumas all in one. Luckily for the rescue party, they had a bit of Leprechaun magic on their side.

Lizzie spun and swung her staff cracking heads and dislocating jaws. The slaves had glazed looks in their eyes and they showed no signs of pain or emotion as the small group slashed, smashed, and thrashed them. Lizzie felt satisfaction as she beat the red-eyes away. After a particularly good Thwack! she chanced a glance at her smaller Leprechaun friends.

Rory was way quicker than he looked. Lizzie thought he looked elvish as fluidly as he darted in and out of stomping feet, firing arrow after arrow into the Ruas. A well-placed arrow would bring down the savage creatures, but Rory didn't always have time to take his best aim. She didn't worry about Rory as she broke the skull of another of Morna's slaves.

Next, she looked up and watched Biddy torment the red-eyes that were still clinging to the ceiling. She darted in and out of their flailing arms and shot daggers from her wings. Bodies splashed all around Lizzie in the shimmering little pool.

"Nice job, Biddy!" she shouted. It gave her strength to see them doing so well, and she knew she had to match them.

Dorian and Brendan stood back-to-back as they faced

the horde. His sword and her magical blasts were making short work of the red-eyes.

After cutting off the head of an ugly female Rua, Brendan took a needed breathe. It seemed like he had been holding it for some time without realizing it. "How are we doing, Dorian?"

Blast!

"Eh, I think we're doing better than they are," she said.

Sching!

"Don't let them fool you," he warned. "They are vicious and will eat you as soon as look at you."

Dorian seared more of the red-eyes from across the cave, cutting their bodies in half. "How do you know anything about them?"

Gorgoch appeared between them. "He's a seer."

"What!" she exclaimed. "You've been having visions and you haven't said anything?"

Brendan sliced and diced and then shrugged. "I didn't know that's what was going on." He blocked a claw and spun out to the right to disembowel the beast. "They have mostly just been dreams, but when we stepped in here, I had one happen right in front on my eyes."

"This one was my fault, I'm afraid," declared Gorgoch with his head hung. "I was relieving a memory, and Brendan must have hitched on to it."

Brendan paused his fight and took a second to pity Gorgoch. If that was how he was caught, then how did he die? he wondered.

"I'm sorry, Artie," replied Brendan.

"It wasn't your doing." Gorgoch's features showed anger and he began to glow with a blue hue. "Don't worry, I won't let them do the same to you."

Dullahan was impressed with the young ones. They were very capable of handling themselves. What pleased him most was how Gorgoch stood, or floated, frozen with fear. This must have been very painful to the spirit man. Dullahan reveled in that.

The Ruas kept coming at the travelers and Dullahan had the feeling that they couldn't hold back the dead for much longer. That was until that blasted spirit exploded. At least that's what it looked like to Dullahan.

The entire cavern was drenched in a bright blue light and in a flash the creatures vanished! Dullahan couldn't believe what had just happened, but whatever it was he had to tell Morna that the travelers were on their way!

"What was that?" asked Lizzie, her eyes still seeing spots.

Dorian looked around with the spots in her vision as well. She saw the spots well, but the Ruas were nowhere to be found. "I–I don't know."

Biddy zoomed down from the ceiling and hovered near Brendan's head. "Where's Artie?"

Brendan thought that the old ghost had something to do with the flash, but he wasn't certain. The fact was the spirit man was gone. It was as if he and the red-eyes had all been teleported somewhere else.

"I don't think we can worry about that right now," said Dorian. "We need to hurry. I feel that my father can't hold out much longer."

"How do you know?" asked Lizzie.

Rory leapt up to her shoulder. "I can feel it, too."

"Then let's get a move on," Brendan declared and walked towards the cave's exit.

✦ ✦ ✦

A dark and shadowed man hovered just out of Oscar's sight, but he knew he was there. He also knew he was still dreaming.

"One down, my friend, and two to go," the shadowed man declared. "You will not remember this conversation, but you will act on my words. Two sisters patiently wait for their discovery, Oscar. You are charged with finding them and returning all three to me."

"Yes," accepted Oscar happily.

"The music box and the prisons of the remaining two shall be brought to me. Do you understand?"

Oscar nodded. "Yes, I understand."

"I've been waiting on you and your children for quite some time. Don't fail me."

The shadowed man vanished as Oscar rolled onto his side. His conscious mind had no recollection of the task that he had been given.

Chapter 16
✝ Specters and Mist ✝

DUNCAN HEARD THE HEEL TAP of boots walk across the floor. He assumed it was Dullahan returning to the tower, but he couldn't be certain. What he did know was that he was in a heap of trouble. He knew he was to his breaking point and the witch was about to get what she wanted.

How did it come to this? How did he let this happen? His thoughts dwelled on his beautiful daughter and the others in his clan that were counting on him. He was about to let them down.

"What is it Dullahan? Why the long face?" cackled Morna, giddy at the prospect of all the magic she was about to capture.

"The slaves have been destroyed, Mistress," Dullahan replied. "They are on their way?"

Morna strolled over to Duncan's cage and smiled. "It won't matter. The Leprechauns will be mine before they arrive."

"And if they are not?"

Morna shrugged. "Then you can kill them."

✦ ✦ ✦

Lizzie and Rory were in the rear of the pack as Dorian and Brendan led the crusade. Biddy flew above them scouting out the path ahead.

They had emerged from the caverns after only a brief time following the battle with the slaves and after Gorgoch had vanished. Brendan wasn't sure if the ghost was coming back or not, but he couldn't worry about that now. He knew that there was a good chance that the Leprechauns who were on his side stood a real chance of jumping ship. Then that would be a huge problem.

"So, tell me about your visions?"

Dorian's question shook him out of his thoughts. He told her about the dream he'd had and about what he had seen in the cave. Reliving the visions made him shudder.

Why had he been able to have visions? What made him special? Or maybe a better questions was what made him cursed?

"Have you ever had a vision before that dream?"

Brendan thought back and he realized that he had. He just didn't recognize it for what it was. He had dreamed about his father before he had a car crash and his mother before she had died. He had seen his grandpa's image from Vietnam even though he had never even met the man before. Little scenes like that had always been with him, only he just explained them away—like saying that he saw these things because he was tired or had a good imagination. Maybe it was something he ate or a conversation that sparked the thought? It wasn't until his Celtic adventure that he realized that some supernatural ability was even a viable explanation to his visions. What a vacation it had turned out to be.

"I'm glad you came with me, Brendan," Dorian said. "I know that I doubted you at the beginning, but you have not only held your own—you've exceeded expectations."

Brendan smiled and glanced over at her. She looked tired and feverish. Her skin was pale and she was sweating, despite the chill in the forest. "Are you alright?"

"I'm fine," she lied. "Let's just get my father back."

"We will. I promise you." Brendan reached down and took her hand in his and they walked through the forest. The trees moved out of their way and Brendan knew it was because of him. He couldn't explain it, but he was feeling stronger, more powerful.

As the forest moved aside, Morna's castle came into view. Brendan steeled his nerves, determined to see it through to the end.

✦ ✦ ✦

Morna saw the group with her own eyes for the first time when they entered the clearing. They had moved through her Black Forest much faster than she had anticipated. The trees should have been doing more to slow them, but that was only a minor concern. She waved her hand through the air and the little bit of water that hung about began to shimmer. An image flashed to life. It was fuzzy at first, but soon enough she could see Duncan's daughter and her friends. She moved the image over so the Leprechaun King could see it as well.

"There she is, Duncan," laughed the witch. "Your precious daughter has arrived to save you."

Duncan's eyelids were heavy and he struggled to open them. He managed to peek through his eyelashes and see the image. The group he saw looked exhausted and frail. How much had they been through on his account? What horrors had they faced?

And then he saw his daughter and his spirit lifted. His eyes opened fully and he struggled to watch. She was holding the hand of a young man that he didn't recognize and she was apparently feeling the affects of Morna's attack on Leprechaun magic. As heartened as he was to see her, he was equally sad to see her suffer.

"Does she look well to you, Duncan?" Morna feigned concern. "The poor dear. Maybe you should help her. You can end her suffering by giving into me."

"How would that help her?" Duncan coughed and wheezed the words out. He wouldn't be able to say anything else for a long time.

"If you cease this senseless resistance, then I will spare your daughter from my control." Morna gave her best smile. "The others in your clan will be mine, but your precious Dorian will be free."

She looked at the little, old Leprechaun to read his response. "What do you say, old friend?"

Duncan tilted his head to see the image again. He reached out for her and the vapor dispersed taking the image away.

"Just something to think about, but don't take too long. The offer won't stand."

✦ ✦ ✦

Gorgoch hovered in the air around the castle. He chose to leave the others because he thought he had a better chance of ending this madness faster if he was on his own. Destroying the Ruas only took a small amount of energy. He would have to admit that he froze at first. Seeing them again had surprised him, but unlike last time he could do something about it. Vaporizing the undead had given him the perfect cover to leave the group and hunt down Morna. Someone had to stop her. He had wanted to all those years ago and it looked like fate was giving him a second chance.

✦ ✦ ✦

The fog was heavy in the air around the tower. Morna

and Dullahan stood near the balcony in silence. The headless demon knew not to speak to the witch unless he was given permission. She was his master. It was she that allowed him to roam the Earth in search of souls. It would remain that way until the witch died or passed ownership on to a new master. He knew his role and he performed his job well.

There was a glint of power in Morna's eyes that was unmistakable. It was greed and ambition. She was going to change the world to her liking and there was nothing that was going to be done about it. She may have looked youthful on the outside, but she had the benefit of centuries of experience. Also, she was a pupil of his former master, Conchar. She knew what she was doing, and it wasn't going to be pretty for the rest of the world.

It surprised Dullahan to see his master's face go from one of satisfied contemplation to one of terror. She clutched at her throat and struggled for a gasp of breath. Her eyes started to bulge as she was lifted into the air and slammed against the far wall with enough force to crack the stone. Dullahan pulled out his hatchet and searched the tower for the assailant, but there was none to be found.

Morna was raked up the wall and smashed into the ceiling. She sprawled against the ceiling and then tumbled through the air until she crashed into the ground. Morna rolled to her feet and thrust her arms out to the sides. A red pulse left her and domed out around the tower. A layer of fog rode the dome and was pinned against the wall. Morna twirled her arm around, and the red pulse raced around the room collecting the fog in a dizzying swirl. The red pulse collected itself at the pinnacle of the tower and shot straight down for the floor. When it hit, a ghostly mass was left unmoving as the red pulse sparked and waved like electrodes.

"A valiant effort, Gorgoch," croaked Morna to the still mass on the stone floor at her feet. "Pity you failed so miserably and your friends are going to either end up as my slaves or suffer a horrible, agonizing death."

The red magic was heavy upon Gorgoch and trapped him despite his best effort to free himself. "I won't let you hurt them!" he declared defiantly.

"Oh, I'm not going to hurt them. You are!"

Morna clenched her fist at Gorgoch and the red magic squeezed in on its prisoner. He screamed at the pain. It was real and cut powerfully at his exposed soul. The red magic absorbed into his body and left him smoking and paralyzed.

"Arise, Gorgoch," Morna commanded. At once Gorgoch rose to an upright position. His eyes were glazed over red, and he stood patiently awaiting his master's desire. "Go and kill your new friends."

Gorgoch faded into smoke and all that could be seen in the vapor were his new red eyes. When they, too, vanished, Morna looked over at Duncan and saw victory was close at hand.

✦ ✦ ✦

"There's the castle. So, how do we get in?" asked Rory.

The structure was mountainous and imposing against the stormy sky. Lightning flashed and thunder boomed just as it should in any scary circumstance. The path led the group to a clearing and to a large misty moat of black water. The drawbridge was up and there was no foreseeable way in.

"Maybe we should knock?" joked Lizzie. "What do you think, Brendan?"

✦ ✦ ✦

The world around him faded out and he was left alone in a white nothingness. He called out for the others, but his echo was the only voice that answered him. He had never felt that alone before. Fear was creeping in on him.

Fear was a dangerous emotion.

He was standing, but he wasn't sure what he was standing on. He couldn't see a surface or a ground. There was no wind and no other stimuli to be processed. Panic was beginning to set in.

"Be calm," commanded a voice.

Instantly, Brendan was overcome with a sense of ease. His breathing slowed and a serenity that should have never been thought of came to him.

"Who's there?" he asked the white nothing.

"Worry not about me, Brendan," commanded the voice. "Your friends are in great peril."

"I already know that," he retorted. He thought about the venom in his reply and continued with more reverence. "I don't know how I can help them."

"You will know when the time is right."

"But what if we are already too late?" he asked.

"There is no such thing," boomed the voice.

Brendan hung his head in confusion and sadness. "I…" his voice faltered.

"When all is lost remember this calm, and then you will realize what has been promised you and your clan."

Brendan looked up, and in a flash he realized that he was still standing in front of Morna's castle and beside his group.

✦ ✦ ✦

"Did you hear me?" Lizzie asked again. "How do we get in?"

"Silence!" yelled Rory as he jumped from Lizzie's shoulder. "Something is here!"

"What's here?" Dorian asked hurriedly.

"I don't know, but it's evil." Rory stalked around with his bow at the ready.

The others braced for combat as well. Lizzie and Dorian stood back to back and inspected the landscape. Biddy hovered above them a helicopter, eagle eyes on full watch.

Brendan was on the look out but the flash vision or visit or whatever it was called weighed on his mind and his attention. What had the voice meant? He was having a hard time not thinking that he had just imagined the voice. People with some forms of dementia heard voices. Maybe that's what he had? For all he knew, he could be in a padded room right now living out some fantasy.

The mist over the black water of the moat began

to bellow out at that point looking a lot like a witch's cauldron. The only thing missing was the howl of a wolf in the distance, but Brendan had no doubt that, too, would happen soon.

Rory prowled near the moat and was absolutely taken off guard when the water reached out and snatched him up like a frog snagging a dopey fly. The little guy was flung straight into the side of the castle and crashed down onto a large rock that barely protruded out of the surface of the water.

"Rory!" screamed Biddy. "I'm coming!"

Biddy dove down to rescue her friend when the mist belched out a bubble and trapped the flying Leprechaun. It floated lazily in the wind and landed somewhere in the distant trees.

"What's going on, Dorian?" screamed Brendan.

"I don't know." She had pulled away from Lizzie and took a few steps back. She slammed into an invisible object and was knocked to the ground. She turned her head in time to see two red eyes appear out of the mist. Her jaw fell open in surprise when Gorgoch solidified before her eyes.

"Artie!" screeched Dorian.

"Death seeks you, Dorian, and I aim to deliver you." Gorgoch opened his mouth and a stream of black mist poured out and surrounded her.

Dorian's hands glowed with her power and she lashed out against the mist. It evaded her touch all the while squeezing in on her.

"Leave her alone!" shouted Lizzie as she swatted at Gorgoch with her staff. The stick passed through him, though, and she lost her balance. Gorgoch made his arm solid and swatted her twenty feet away. She crashed to the ground and rolled. She didn't move when her rolling ended.

"You son of a—" Brendan slashed down with his sword and chopped off the solid arm. It fell away and turned to black mist when it hit the ground. Instantly, a new arm reformed itself out of Gorgoch's shoulder, only this time it carried a sword as well.

"Fool," chastised the spirit. "You have already lost."

Gorgoch lashed out with his sword, and Brendan easily countered and parried in return. They exchanged attacks with neither gaining an advantage.

"After I kill you, boy, I will finish off your sister and your girlfriend." Gorgoch's red eyes were like fire and his white glow had been overrun with a red pulsation.

"Come on, Artie," pleaded Brendan. "We're your friends."

"Wrong. My only friend is death. I would like to introduce you."

Gorgoch struck high and Brendan easily blocked the blow. He then spun and dipped even lower only to bring his blade up into the center of the spirit's chest. To his surprise the blade speared the ghost like any other man. Gorgoch's surprised face told Brendan that he had found his mark.

Gorgoch's arm returned to mist, but his body remained

lodged on the end of Brendan's blade. The black mist around Dorian vanished in the wind and she got to her feet and stumbled to Brendan's side.

Gorgoch opened his mouth to speak, but it was obvious that they weren't his words. "Fools! You are too late. Duncan's power will be my own and then I will be unstoppable!"

Dorian had tears reach her eyes. "Let my father go!"

Morna looked through a patch of mist, seeing through Gorgoch's eyes. She looked out at the American and the princess.

"Little girl, what makes you think that you can command me?"

"You could have lived and served in my new world, as meager as that existence would have been, but I have made your protector your destroyer," Gorgoch continued the speech for his master.

The spirit man's eyes assumed a sharper and bloodier red. Though he was still impaled on Brendan's sword, he reached out and began to choke both Brendan and Dorian. Gorgoch thrust Dorian away and nearly into the water. He wanted to focus his rage on Brendan.

"Your pitiful toy can't stop me, boy!" he taunted.

Brendan tightened his grip on the sword and somehow started to calm his mind. The magical sword responded to Brendan and radiated more power. Gorgoch's elusive expression told the tale, and he released his grip on Brendan. The power of the sword pushed the ghost back to the very tip.

Dorian ran back to Brendan's side. "Don't destroy him! He's not in control."

She reached out and placed her hand on Brendan's, and her energy crackled up the blade until it met Gorgoch's chest. The ghost was sent like a rocket out of the Black Forest and away from the witch. Dorain and Brendan fell to the ground sweating and exhausted.

"I couldn't let you destroy him," she wheezed. "He's our friend."

"Sorry. He wasn't leaving me much choice."

Biddy had already freed herself from the tangled branches and bubble residue and scooped up Rory. Lizzie got to her feet and hobbled back to the group.

"Now what?" Lizzie asked.

"Now we finish this," declared Dorian.

Chapter 17

✝ The Calm ✝

MORNA WAS NOT AT ALL HAPPY after Gorgoch was flung out of the woods as if he had been shot from a cannon. The one bright side was that the Leprechaun magic was much more powerful than she had first thought. At least that made the eventual outcome all the more worth the hassle of these little fools.

The time for playing had passed. She never thought they would make it to her gate in one piece, so it was time to unleash her hellish terror.

She turned to Dullahan. "Destroy the Leprechauns and the girl."

Dullahan bowed. "It will be done. What of the boy?"

Morna smiled cruelly. "Don't worry. My pet will take care of him." She stroked the griffin's feathers gently as lightning flashed in her eyes.

The griffin gained a little momentum in a jog and jumped into the darkened sky as the first raindrops began to fall. Lightning flashed and the griffin closed its eyes. It flapped hard to rise higher and higher and when it got several hundred meters above the ground it peered down with exceptional vision for its prey. Once it spotted the swordsman, it let out a triumphant screech and pulled its wings straight back and dove for the ground. The rain stung on its face and splashed off of its beak, but the griffin narrowed its gaze and honed in on the boy.

The thunder clapped and Lizzie jumped in response. She hated storms to begin with, but she especially hated them in a cursed forest outside of a frightening castle. She hated the fact that they didn't have a way in.

"So, how are we getting in?" she asked.

Rory and Biddy exchanged glances. "I think I've got an idea," he said.

Rory shot two arrows at the same time and they found

their mark on the top two corners of the drawbridge. Long strings of magic remained tethered to the shafts and connected the arrows with the bow. Rory tossed the strings up to Biddy and snatched them up and pushed against the air with a mighty flap. She struggled at first and Lizzie thought the little Leprechaun was wasting her time when the drawbridge began to pull away from the wall.

"No way!" Lizzie shouted in excitement.

"Come on, Bid," encouraged Rory.

The little Leprechaun kept on pulling and slowly brought the gargantuan door down to the ground. It made a loud thud, and Biddy dropped the strings and shook the wear out of her hands.

"Great job, Biddy!" everyone shouted and cheered as the first raindrops splattered.

✦ ✦ ✦

The griffin was silent and used the storm to hide its approach. The raindrops around it were huge and shaped like mini torpedos. The griffin cut right through them in a direct path for the boy. It made minor adjustments as the swordsman and his group were starting to cross the drawbridge.

Just before the griffin reached the boy, it stretched out its claws and opened them wide just like it would while on the hunt for prey. The moment arrived and the griffin shrieked in excitement and wrapped its talons around the boy. It's left talon wrapped up his left arm and its right talon snatched the boy across his right shoulder and around his chest. If the griffin could have smiled it would have as it took to the air and left the others behind.

"Noooooo!" shouted Lizzie. She chased after the rising griffin for a few steps until it and Brendan became a dot in the sky. Seconds later they vanished amongst the clouds.

She slumped her shoulders and felt absolutely defeated. She dropped to her knees and tears ran out of her eyes. Dorian placed her hand on Lizzie's head.

"He'll be fine, Lizzie," she said.

"How do you know that?" Lizzie cried.

Dorian didn't know it. She wanted to believe it, though, and that had to be enough. "You need to have faith in him."

"We need to go in and stop that witch, now!" warned Rory. "Our time is short. Can't you feel it?"

No one answered, but they knew he was right.

Lizzie got to her feet, but she refused to wipe the tears away. They were going to fuel her. She had something more to fight for now and that witch and her lackies were going to pay for it. Lizzie stalked across the drawbridge and the others followed. Whatever lay ahead had better be ready.

I should have seen it coming, Brendan thought as he soared away from his sister and the Leprechauns. *What was the point of being a seer if you can't even see the danger that you're in?*

He was shaken and woozy from the sudden ascension, but the nausea was beginning to subside and he started to take inventory of the situation. The first thing he realized was that the griffin could drop him at any moment and he would plunge to his death. That was not a comforting thought, so the idea of slicing into the thing's leg with his sword was out. He also realized that he had a huge pain in his left side. The pain was stinging, but the cold air was making it difficult to know if it was his side or the wind that was causing the pain. He guessed it was a little of both.

The griffin soared higher and higher and eventually reached the edge of the Black Forest. It curled its path and just skimmed the boundary of the black storm clouds. Brendan had a feeling that it didn't want to leave the cover of the storm. Bits of icy rain began pelting his face and he squinted his eyes against it.

What was this overgrown buzzard going to do with him?

✦ ✦ ✦

Dorian stepped ahead of Lizzie and through the entrance. She scanned the great entrance hall and spotted nothing. There was a stone staircase on the far left that spiraled up and away into the darkened space overhead and down into a rectangular opening in the floor. The room wasn't as gloomy as Dorian had expected. There were plenty of lit torches hanging in the chandeliers. There was no furniture or paintings. Nothing that was inviting or charming. It was just empty and Dorian thought that was about right considering the black-hearted owner of the place.

"Where do you think she's keeping him?" asked Biddy,

two feet off to Dorian's left.

"My guess is up or down," answered Lizzie gesturing with her staff.

Dorian had considered the same. She knew that they were going to have to split up if they stood any chance of finding her father. She heaved out a long breath and made a decision. "Okay. We'll have to split up." The others were silent, but she could read the concern on their faces. "You three go down and I'll go up."

Biddy protested first. "You can't go on your own!"

"You need one of us to watch your back, Dorian!" agreed Rory.

Lizzie listened to the others but she cleared her throat and shook her head. "She's right. She can look out for herself, but we are going to need each other." The others stared back at her. She didn't miss a beat and turned to go down the stairwell.

Dorian nodded at Biddy and Rory and they followed her down. Dorian slowed her breathing in an attempt to slow her heart rate, but it didn't help. She climbed the steps with her hands glowing and her eyes scanning.

Chapter 18

✜ The Storm ✜

THE GRIFFIN'S SCREECH was piercing. The abomination flew him around and around as if searching for just the right kill spot. He lost track of how long he was in its clutches, but he wasn't looking forward to when he wasn't.

Apparently, the beast had found what it was looking

for and it pulled hard with its massive and powerful wings, arching momentarily before plunging into a dive. Brendan's gut tightened and jumped into his chest just like it did on every rollercoaster he had ever ridden. This time, though, there would be no sudden turn before he hit the ground. He peered through the rushing wind and ice pellets and located the dumb beast's kill spot.

The griffin had angled them so that they were approaching the Black River, only this stretch of water had unnatural jagged rocks that were protruding out of the current. The stones were black like obsidian, but they were huge with serrated sides. It was not Brendan's ideal landing zone.

"Can't we talk about this?" he screamed above the noise. The griffin did not reply.

✦ ✦ ✦

Morna took the obsidian dagger out and held it with reverence. Soon the dagger would help fulfill the plans that Conchar had shared with her before he disappeared. Though the blade was black, she perceived the dark shadow that her mentor had set upon it and the blurry, golden vision of a second shadow. She still didn't know the purpose of the golden image, but it hardly mattered. She would soon fulfill her portion of the plan, and with Conchar gone, she would take his piece of the pie as well. Soon, she could set her magical and horrific army on the world, but first she had these pesky travelers to deal with.

✦ ✦ ✦

Lizzie, Rory, and Biddy cautiously hurried down the

stairs. They knew that time was drawing short, but they were also aware that they were in an evil witch's castle, so to hurry cautiously seemed like a nice balance.

It didn't take them long to find the end of the stairs. They never found any other entrances except for the one at the very bottom. The faint glow of torches illuminated the doorframe and the bottom three stairs. Walking through the doorway they entered into a huge and very open hall that had several doors, both wooden and barred, lining it.

"Shall we pick a door?" asked Rory.

Lucky for them––or unlucky for them––all the doors opened at once negating the need to select one. Opened, though, is not strong enough of a word. The doors exploded off the hinges and flew about the hall smashing into other doors and into the walls. Splinters and shards were thrown about, but the protective glow of the magic they had absorbed deflected the fragments.

Once the sawdust settled, Lizzie took inventory of what had just happened. "Whoa! That was crazy!"

Rory and Biddy nodded, but when the pitch-black rooms became alight with glowing red eyes, they knew that the craziness was just about to be multiplied.

Dorian hummed to herself as she ascended the stairs. She often did that when she was nervous. She had only been this nervous once before. She was very young when her mother became ill and on her last night on the Earth, Dorian was ushered to her bed side. She was nervous because once her mother was gone, it was going to be left to her to take care of her father. That was a lot of pressure for a kid. Couple that with the responsibilities of being the heir to the crown and you have one tall order. It wasn't that her father was stupid or careless, but he was naïve and that had always scared her mother. That anxiety was passed on to daughter and was at an all-time high as she climbed each new step.

She knew in her heart that her father was being held in the tower. It seemed unlikely that at the very moment of gaining all of the Leprechaun magic that she would want to be in the dungeon. No, the witch had to have an ego to want to steal the power for her own in the first place, so that would have to place her in the tower. A good bet would also be on her father being in the tower too so she could gloat and celebrate in her evil.

The thoughts both scared and infuriated her. She knew the witch was powerful, but she also knew that she wasn't about to let her father die without a fight. The old witch didn't know what was coming her way.

✦ ✦ ✦

The rocks of sure death were fast approaching and Brendan had no idea how to stop the descent. The griffin on the other hand knew just how to stop itself from slamming into the rocks. It released Brendan on a direct trajectory towards the jagged stones some five hundred feet above the ground.

Brendan screamed as the creature arched away. The wind rushed by as the ground rushed forward. Brendan focused on the stones and then his mind swiftly moved to thoughts of his father and sister and a million memories of his life back in America. The clichéd life flashing before his eyes was pretty disappointing and really boring. He was disappointed all the way until the memories landed in Ireland. The crazy events he had experienced with the rescue party flew by, and he watched them with amazement. Amazement because he was actually a part of them. His last one was of the panic stricken faces of Lizzie and Dorian. That's where his focus held and that's why he failed to notice the silver energy spread from the blade up through the hilt and into his arm. His entire body radiated the silver glow by the time he smashed into the serrated rocks.

✦ ✦ ✦

The red-eyes emerged from the darkened doors and advanced into the hall. Dozens of gaunt-looking fairies trailed the zombie-like slaves and hovered above them with nasty little grins through black lips and gray, sunken cheeks. Everybody around Rory, Biddy, and Lizzie was drooling and smelled like rotting bacon.

"Be ready, lasses, this is going to get ugly," warned Rory.

"It's already ugly, Rory," joked Biddy in a weak attempt to cut her nerves down.

The Ruas stood around the perimeter of the three waiting while the Sidhes flapped their leathery wings. They were waiting for something, but Lizzie couldn't imagine what it was. She didn't have to wait long because a slightly larger and even more deranged looking Sidhe burst out of a black room and spread his wings wide to slow his flight.

"Oh no!" cried Biddy. "It's Wardicon."

"Wardicon?" asked Lizzie, her purple staff humming in her hands.

"The Sidhe King," answered Rory.

The king surveyed the small group that his Sidhes and the Ruas confronted. He growled and then spat out his command. It wasn't a complicated directive. He simply said, "Kill!"

✦ ✦ ✦

Dorian reached the tower entrance with her heart pounding so loudly in her chest that she was pretty sure the witch could hear her coming. She cautiously peered around the corner and into the room. It was humongous compared to what she thought it was going to be. From the base of the castle the tower looked tiny. Looks were definitely deceiving.

The tower was apparently the base of operations. Morna had a large stone table that somewhat resembled an altar with four obsidian chairs placed around it. A dagger of the same black stone was laid across the table with bits of gore still clinging to it. Dorian crept beside it hiding herself between the altar and the wall. She nearly puked at the sight of the bloody tissue hanging on the blade. She crept a little further on and looked out in the middle of the great room. There were the mutilated bodies of four Ruas lying about, probably the source of the gore on the blade.

The balcony was lit by the lightning and was taking on

rain. She didn't see her father anywhere in the tower. Had she picked the wrong direction?

She looked at her glowing hands and thought. She flicked her fingers and sprayed tiny sparks of red toward the center of the room. "Go," she commanded. "Find my father."

The tiny balls of red light floated like lightning bugs around the room. Some soared into the rafters while the others darted in and out of dark spaces in the tower. Finally, they all converged on a damp, shadowed area in the north corner. They settled in the base of a wrought iron cage and glowed.

Dorian's breath caught in her throat. Her father was there, but he looked terrible. Death couldn't be far behind, or maybe something worse than death––like being Morna's pawn. Duncan's head turned slightly and he mouthed her name.

Dorian lost her head. She stood up and cried out. "Father! I'm here!"

She began to run across the room, closing the distance between herself and the cage. Her footsteps were so loud on the stone floor. Time slowed, or maybe she did. It was taking an impossibly long time to get there. She was caught off guard when a black figure seamlessly slipped out of the shadows and impeded her path. She skidded to a stop at Dullahan's feet and fell on her backside. She looked up at the demon.

"I'm here, too, Your Highness," bellowed the headless one.

Chapter 19
✚ Sacrifice ✚

A PRESENCE ENVELOPED all of the Gaelic kingdoms and observed. The balance of magic was nearly warped by the witch, but somehow the little Leprechaun was hanging on. It was doubtful that Duncan would be able to last much longer, though. The presence thought about how interesting the entire scene was and wondered how it would end. Could the witch pull off the coup of magic or would this unlikely group, which the presence had set in motion, come through? It had been so long since the presence had involved himself in the affairs of man. The last time he did he lost his mortal life. He couldn't let the humans down again. The boy's birthright was the only chance the world had. It was in his hands now.

✦ ✦ ✦

Flashes of orange, blue, and purple slammed into the attacking red-eyes and Sidhes. Lizzie's staff crushed the skull of a female Rua and, just before it crumpled to the ground, Lizzie gave it a front kick and sent it into four other gray-skins.

Biddy's blue wings shone brilliantly in the dim lighting of the hall. She zoomed in and out of the cantankerous leathery bat-like freaks. They slashed at her, but she evaded the attempts. Sharp barbs flew from her wings and knocked several of the Sidhes to the floor. Some of them were pinned to the ground, while others limped along the ground with holes sliced into their wings. They pumped their fists at her in anger, but were relatively powerless to do anything about it.

Rory shot his arrows like Robin Hood and darted in and out of stomping feet. He kept a wary eye on the Sidhe King because he had not attacked yet. He shot a final arrow into the eye of an unfortunate Rua when he noticed a change in Wardicon.

The Sidhe King dropped to the floor and convulsed.

He wretched and vomited out black ooze before his body convulsed and he rolled onto his back. He screamed in pain as his body swelled and bulged. His hands and feet extended and long grizzled claws forced their way out of his fingertips. His pointy ears protruded further. His facial features grew more contorted and grotesque. When he had finally stopped howling and changing, Wardicon stood to his full height, which was over seven feet tall at this point, and fixed his eyes on the ones with the colorful magic.

"Holy crap," observed Lizzie.

Wardicon howled ferociously and snatched up a Rua who had stumbled too close to him. He used both hands and tore the undead in half and chucked the halves at Rory, Biddy, and Lizzie.

"Okay," swallowed Lizzie. "That has to be the grossest thing I've ever seen."

Wardicon took two steps forward and strained his now very developed and corded muscles. He opened his jaws and roared and salivated.

"What do we do?" shouted Biddy.

"Run!" answered Rory.

And they did.

They ran back to the stairwell knocking red-eyes and Sidhes out of the way. They took the steps two at a time and ran as fast as they could up the spiraled staircase. They ran faster when they heard Wardicon hit the first step.

✦ ✦ ✦

"Stupid, little girl," Dullahan provoked. "Did you think

that you were going to stop us?" A frightening, hollow laugh echoed out of the hole where his head should have been.

Dorian crab-walked backwards as Dullahan advanced and raised his sword. He slammed it down and struck nothing but stone. A spray of sparks lit the air as Dorian flipped out of the way. She turned on the spot and blasted Dullahan with a lightning bolt of red energy in the chest. He fell backwards and skidded on his back. His chest smoldered and smoked, but he was hard to defeat and sat upright.

"Why don't you just die?" Dorian cried.

"You first, Princess."

Dullahan sprung to his feet, charged forward, and slashed out with his sword as he pulled his ax from its loop. They found the surface of a red shield that formed in front of Dorian. The impacts were fierce and powerful. The first one drove her to her knees. The second was an uppercut and sent Dorian across the room until she landed on the altar and slid into one of the chairs knocking them to the ground. She hit her head in multiple places and she was seeing stars, but Dullahan's heavy boot steps brought her back to her sense in a hurry. He jumped on top of the altar and began to bring his ax down upon her. She blasted the chair, and it flew into Dullahan, crashing him to the stone floor.

She had bought herself a little time to think. What should she do? How do you defeat a demon? She glanced around and saw that the contents of her bag had spilled out. What caught her eye was the small container of the golden dust of the force field residue. She lifted the vile and dumped it into her palms. Her body was overcome with a golden glow and she stood up. There was no way she was going to be able to hid when she shown like a candle.

"It doesn't matter what color your magic is, girl. You can't beat me." Dullahan twirled the ax in his left hand and strode forward.

Dorian took a deep breathe and jumped on top of the alter. "Bring it."

✦ ✦ ✦

The griffin circled over the Black River and screeched triumphantly. It peered down into the mist and dust to find the swordsman's body. It flew lower and searched. It needed to confirm that the boy was dead. Morna would not be too forgiving if the swordsman were to show up again.

The griffin landed on the banks of the Black River with soft feet. It walked closer to the water and stared down into the current. It's own reflection looked back at it. It snorted and sniffed and was pretty satisfied that the swordsman was dead. It leaned over and lapped at the water. Killing people was a thirsty business.

Water dripped off its beak and made ripples in the river. It began to walk away and take to the air when bubbles rose to the surface. The griffin stopped and looked over its shoulder. It was just one or two bubbles at first, but the griffin knew that magic was hard to destroy. It came back and readied itself for a fight. It pulled its paw back and spread its claws. The bubbles came up faster and larger until it looked like the river was boiling.

A silver magic was obvious in the river, and the griffin growled. Brendan burst from the water, throwing energy from his body without even thinking about it. He searched around and then spotted the beast on the banks with its mouth hanging open in surprise.

He stared at the griffin and its eyes took on a silver glaze. Brendan, whose body was shining brightly, walked out of the water and mounted the griffin.

"Back to the castle," he said, tapping his heels on its sides. The griffin sprang into the air. "I hope we're not too late."

✦ ✦ ✦

"Get outside!" screamed Lizzie, leading the sprint.

She and the Leprechauns made their way across the drawbridge and across the moat. Wardicon wasn't far behind and once he hit the openness of the outdoors, he took to the skies and surged at his enemies.

Rory fell onto his back and shot his arrows into Wardicon's eyes. Temporally blinded, the large, mutated Sidhe crashed into the ground and slid into a tree.

"Great shot, Rory!" complimented Biddy.

They crossed onto the land and became ready. Wardicon blinked the orange arrows out of his eyes and wiped the wetness from them. He glared at the group and snarled.

It was frightening and nightmarish. Lizzie wanted to

wet herself, but didn't think it would help any. She would just be wet and scared instead of just scared.

"We need to stick together and move. No one sits still for long," strategized Biddy. "You strike and then you move and the next one takes a shot."

"Maybe he'll wear out," offered Rory.

"Or maybe it will just make him angrier," suggested Lizzie.

"Either way it's better than just letting him rip us to shreds." Biddy flapped her wings and narrowed her gaze. "Here we go."

Wardicon took to the air and roared. He flapped hard and rose high above them. Biddy zipped up to confront him and fired barbs in rapid succession pelting the Sidhe king. They did little more than annoy the creature like the thorns of a rose, but it was effective in drawing his attention. He pulled up short of crashing down on Lizzie and Rory and went after Biddy instead. She was a fast flyer, though, so she was not an easy catch.

Rory took the opportunity to fire several arrows into the beast's buttocks. Wardicon stopped in mid-air and shot a hateful look back at the archer.

"Run, Rory!" screamed Lizzie.

Rory ran and Wardicon pursued, swooping low and stretching out his claws to snatch the annoying little Leprechaun up. Lizzie started swatting stones from the banks at Wardicon. A few actually hit the big lug.

"Hey, ugly!" she taunted. "Come pick on someone your own size."

As soon as the words left her mouth, she regretted it. He changed courses and headed directly at her. She was fast, but she wasn't fast enough to escape him. He slashed down, and she went into defensive mode blocking his arm with the staff. The contact with the staff burned Waridcon's flesh and he retracted his arm quickly. He howled and slashed out again, only this time without trying to make contact.

They circled each other and Lizzie was scared to death. This was a nightmare come true and she had to hold her ground. She couldn't run. She couldn't hide. She had to make a stand.

Wardicon had his back to the moat and cocked his head at Lizzie. He leaned his head back and howled at the water. For a moment, the tension was the only thing boiling in sight, but suddenly the water started to churn and a large water beast shot out of the water and landed at Wardicon's side.

"Heavens!" cried Biddy. "It's Usis!"

Usis the Merrow Queen had mutated as well. Her once beautiful features were gone, replaced by the mangled and demonic characteristics of a dragon. To Lizzie she looked like the Loch Ness Monster on steroids.

Usis climbed onto land, towering over Wardicon. Black water rolled on her back and fell in drops onto the grass.

"Talk about out of the frying pan and into the fire," observed Rory.

✦ ✦ ✦

Dullahan ran at Dorian and swiped his sword at her

ankles, but met nothing but air as she catapulted herself into the air and flipped over the headless demon. In mid-air she couldn't help but glance down into his neck, but there was nothing to see except for swirling black smoke. She assumed it was his essence or his blackened, evil soul. Either way, she didn't want to see it again.

She landed and sent flames of red at Dullahan's back. His cape was consumed, but he simply tore it away and threw it aside.

"Why do you delay the inevitable?" he asked. "In a few short minutes, your clan's magic with be Morna's and you will be her slave."

"That is tempting, but I think I'd rather keep my mind and my magic, thank you very much."

"Suit yourself. Time to die." The demon closed in on her and lashed out with his sword and ax, battering at her protective golden shield.

She felt each blow as if being hit while inside a punching bag. She held her arms out instinctively as he struck her with each blow. She was knocked left and right; her head was ringing from the onslaught. He side kicked her in the chest and skipped her body across the floor. She came to rest next to her father's cage.

She looked at him through woozy, belabored eyes. "Father," she whispered.

"Oh, how touching," hissed a voice from across the room.

Dorian looked over and watched Morna cross the tower floor. She stopped and stood above the fallen princess and the weakened king. "Is this reunion all that you hoped it would be?"

Dorian held her hand out and put it into the cage. She rubbed her father's arm with her finger. "Let him go."

"Ha!" cackled the witch. "Give up, child. You've been defeated. Your little Leprechaun friends and the girl are just about to die, your spirit friend has turned on you, and my griffin has destroyed your insignificant boyfriend." She stared hard into Dorian's eyes. "All hope is lost."

Lightning flashed and thunder clashed and Brendan, riding atop the griffin flew through the window, much to Morna's surprise.

"All hope lost?" He jumped from the griffin's back, executing three perfect flips, and landed in front of Dorian. "I don't think so."

Morna glared at the griffin and spat, "How could you betray me?"

"It really wasn't his fault. I'm just too dang charming," said Brendan. He nodded and the griffin flew from the tower.

He hacked down with his sword on the cage's lock. "Take your father and go. I'll handle this."

"Who do you think you are?" Morna screamed.

Brendan fixed her with a stare and recognition beset her eyes. She knew who he was or at least from where his power came. "It's too late, boy. The Leprechaun magic is mine."

"We'll see about that, witch."

"You will lose," she croaked.

Brendan looked over at Dullahan. "I think she's talking to you, handsome."

Dullahan took a tighter grip on his ax and sword. "You talk too much for someone who's about to die."

"You talk too much for someone without a head. Seriously, that's creepy."

Dullahan roared and attacked. Brendan was more than ready and rushed to meet the challenge. Metal clanged on metal. Demon strength met resistance from some newfound strength within the American. Strike for strike, the boy parried and blocked and was up to the challenge. It didn't matter if the headless demon used the ax or the blade, the boy countered. Brendan sidestepped a frontal attack and spun into the air and placed a roundhouse kick squarely into the demon's sternum. Dullahan flew backwards and skidded into the middle of the tower floor.

In the meantime, Dorian reached inside the cage and lifted Duncan out. She got to her feet and began to limp across the room. Morna blasted Dorian with an enormous amount of energy from the middle of the room. Dorian was smashed into the wall and pinned there until she collapsed unconsciously to the ground. Duncan fell from her arms and bounced off the floor.

Wardicon and Usis advanced on Rory, Biddy, and Lizzie. This was not at all what Lizzie had in mind when her father suggested going to Ireland for a little family time. He never said anything about dying during a quest.

"This may be the last time I have a chance to say this,"

began Rory. "But I love you, Biddy."

"I love you, too, Rory," she gushed. "Why did we waste so much time in our lives ignoring what was right in front of us?"

"I don't know, but at least if we die, we'll die with love in our heart," he finished.

"I think that's sweet and all, but let's focus less on the dying part and more on getting through this," suggested Lizzie. "You two take the dragon and I'll take Wardicon."

Wardicon ran at the group and Lizzie ran forward to meet him. She spun her staff in front of her to make it hard for Wardicon to reach her. He didn't bother. Instead, he tackled her and broke her magical staff in two. He drove her into the ground and rolled end over end with her in his clutches. His momentum took him to his feet and he flung her towards the trees.

Biddy and Rory cried out in horror, but to their amazement, the griffin swooped out of nowhere and snatched her out of the sky. She hung limply in its clutches as it brought her gently to the ground, laying her by her companions.

Wardicon leapt into the air and the griffin jumped up to challenge him. Rory and Biddy looked at each other. Both shrugged and looked back at Usis.

She advanced and roared, snapping her jaws with the full intention of devouring the Leprechauns. Rory started firing his arrows and Biddy shot daggers at the beast, but that did little more than make it sneeze. Usis began to lunge at the pair but pulled up short.

The Leprechauns looked at one another again.

"Your magic is fading, Bid," Rory pointed out.

"Your's, too, love," she replied.

They each fell to the ground while their consciousness began to slip away.

✦ ✦ ✦

"Do me a favor, Duncan, and get on with it," Morna commanded to the small heap on the floor.

On command, Duncan convulsed and grew paler. His limbs stiffened, and his face contorted. The last of his will broke and the magic that was in his charge left him.

Morna breathed in the cool air in the tower as she absorbed the final energies from the fallen king of the Leprechauns. She looked down at Duncan and smirked. He wasn't moving.

"Hmmm. It looks as though you have outlived your usefulness, Duncan." Morna levitated Duncan to the altar and then glanced back at Dorian. "Well, Duncan, since your next in line is already here and in my possession, I no longer need you."

Duncan roused a little, his features mostly staying his own, and looked over at the witch. Morna reached down and snatched the dagger from the surface of the altar and looked at it admiringly. She sent a charge of magic through the weapon, released it, and made it hover above the little king. "Good-bye, Duncan. It's been a real blast."

She drove the dagger down and slammed it into the center of Duncan's chest. The energy incinerated the unfortunate king, leaving behind ashes that were blown from the table by the wind.

Chapter 20

+ Strength Within +

A HUGE FLASH OF ENERGY caught Brendan's eye during his battle with Dullahan. He felt the power shift in the room and he knew what had happened.

"My master has won, fool," taunted Dullahan. "Give up."

"Go to hell!" demanded Brendan.

Dullahan charged forward, but Brendan was infuriated. He didn't even bother to raise his sword at the advancing demon, instead choosing to lift a single hand causing Dullahan to freeze in mid-stride. If he would have had a face, Brendan was sure that he would have seen absolute shock on it.

"Let me help you get there." Brendan sent Dullahan straight into the wall and the demon vanished in a cloud of smoke.

He turned back to Morna and cocked his head to one side and cracked his neck. Morna stood near the altar, smiling with her arms folded into her robes.

"What now, boy?" she asked. "Do you expect to defeat me when I have the power of the Merrows, the Sidhes, and the Leprechauns added to my own? It's laughable!" She plucked the obsidian dagger from the altar and blew the ashes away from the edge.

"What makes you think that all that magic's going to save you?" asked Brendan to her surprise.

The witch cackled again. Brendan couldn't help but think about the Wizard of Oz. He doubted water was going to melt this witch, though.

"I think I'll let my new slave take care of you." She flicked her finger in Dorian's direction and instantly she began to change. She rose to her feet a mutated form of herself.

When Dorian was fully upright, she turned to face Brendan. She had porcelain skin and pointy fangs that protruded from her lips. Her eyes were gold and her hair had a mind of its own, as if she was floating underwater. She had black claws at the ends of her boney fingers. She resembled the scariest goth chick ever. Brendan was always a little afraid of those girls back at home. He never quite knew why until this moment.

"Quite fetching, isn't she?" Morna said laughing. She turned to Dorian. "Queen Dorian, destroy your betrothed."

"Betrothed?" asked Brendan in surprise.

Dorian charged forward with her fangs bared and claws slashing. Brendan dodged and moved but didn't strike back. Dorian was way quicker than he remembered, though, and she caught his cheek with a left claw. Hot, painful blood dripped down out of the wound. She also threw kicks and punches and objects at him. She even released a pulse of red energy, and it drove him into the altar, causing it to tip over. His weight, making it tip forward, tilted the opposite end into the air.

"Owww," he said.

Dorian was relentless and ran in and kicked him in the chest causing the altar to slide into the wall. The legs of the altar came off like shrapnel. She kicked again, but this time he caught her foot and flipped her away from him. She crashed to the floor, but quickly sprang to her feet.

"Give it up, witch, before you are destroyed." Brendan kept one eye on Dorian and one on Morna. The witch was content to watch Dorian do her dirty work.

"What do you owe the Leprechauns, boy?"

"My name is Brendan," he replied in a shout. "I think

you should know who's going to defeat you."

"You mean your name is Nuada, don't you?" she grinned maliciously.

Brendan didn't have a clue as to what she was talking about, nor the time to respond because Dorian was on him in a second. She grabbed him and hoisted him into the air and flung him across the room towards the balcony. She ran and grabbed him by the throat off of the floor and arched him over the railing. She was strong and held him in place.

Morna stepped into Brendan's line of sight and stood in front of the altar. She flipped the obsidian dagger in the air like a chef. "Looks like Nuada's chosen warrior has failed just as he did long ago."

"What are you talking about?" grunted Brendan.

"So long, Brendan. Thanks for making this all so exciting."

The witch held the dagger by the handle and hurled it end over end at Brendan's face. Brendan pushed Dorian away and spun to the left. He reached out with his right hand and snatched the dagger out of the air by the handle. He rotated it back to his right and let the dagger fly back at Morna. The witch was so surprised that the dagger had penetrated her chest through the heart and pinned her to the altar before she recognized what had happened.

Dorian made to attack but collapsed to the floor. Brendan ignored her for the moment and stalked cautiously towards Morna.

"I warned you," he said.

Blood trickled out of the corner of Morna's mouth and fell onto her robes. Despite the fact that she was dying, she smiled. "Something worse is coming, Nuada's champion, and you have wrought it upon this world. I see now what my master had planned." She was lost for the briefest of moments in reverie before turning her dying attention to Brendan. "Prepare yourself for war."

Brendan allowed her to hang limply on the dagger and ran over to Dorian's side. He turned her over and held her head. The pale color darkened to her normal skin tone, her fangs receded into her mouth, and her black claws retreated into her fingers as everything went back to normal.

"Dorian?"

She moved slightly and her eyelids fluttered opened. "What… what happened?"

Brendan pursed his lips at what he was going to have to tell her. "It's over."

He helped her get to a sitting position and brushed the hair out of her eyes. She stared up at him and asked, "My father?"

Brendan shook his head and pulled her close when she began to cry. He held her tightly because he felt the waves of pain coming off of her. "Even after the power left him, he was never really hers, Dorian. That's why she killed him." With tear filled eyes, she looked up. "He died because she couldn't break him."

She smiled weakly and laid her head upon his chest.

Chapter 21
✢ Homecoming ✢

A FEW MINUTES LATER Rory, Biddy, and Lizzie flew in through the balcony atop of the griffin. Wardicon, who had also returned to his old form, followed them inside.

Lizzie got down quickly and ran over to hug Brendan and Dorian. "I thought I'd lost you!" she cried.

"I'm like a bad penny, Liz. I always turn up."

"I don't even know what that means, but I don't care." Lizzie realized at that moment how much her brother meant to her, but there was no way in the world that she was going to let him know it—especially not in public. She pulled out of the hug and slugged him on the arm. "Don't ever scare me like that again, stupid."

"Ouch," he said with a knowing smile while he rubbed his arm.

They were joined by Rory and Biddy as Wardicon and the griffin watched from a respectful distance.

Wardicon landed softly near the group hug and cleared his throat. "I must offer my thanks to you all and especially to your father. Usis sends her regards as well."

Dorian nodded. "He hung on bravely, but in the end…" her voice trailed off.

"I know he's gone, but without him delaying the witch, you would have never made it here to foil her plans." Wardicon looked at her with wise eyes. "It's hard to understand, but he will be remembered as a hero. That is his legacy."

Brendan nodded and Wardicon nodded in return and took to the skies. "My Sidhes await my return. Know that we are at your beck and call, Queen Dorian." The Sidhe King took to the air and flew off the balcony.

They waved goodbye and watched as the magic they had absorbed faded away.

"Huh," laughed Biddy, landing gracefully on the stone floor after her wings were gone. "Looks like the magic held up just long enough."

Rory's bow vanished. Lizzie's staff turned to a haze of purple smoke. Dorian's red glow and gold shield blinked out of existence. Only Brendan's sword remained.

"No fair!" protested Lizzie. "Why does he get to keep his?"

Brendan leaned in close to Lizzie and whispered. "Because I'm cool like that."

She slugged him again.

When Dorian had recovered enough, the group mounted the griffin and took to the skies. Gorgoch caught up with them somewhere between Scotland and Ireland.

"I see that you prevailed," he said as his features shifted to something like a smile.

"It was at a cost," replied Dorian. "My father was lost to us."

"Take it from me, Dorian; he's never really gone."

"Thanks for all your help, Artie," said Brendan.

Gorgoch stared at him for a moment and then nodded. "You're welcome. Something's different about you, my friend." Brendan didn't quite understand, and his face must have shown it. "Just be careful." Gorgoch faded from sight.

Dorian glanced at Brendan. "What was he talking about?"

"I don't know," he replied. Before he had too much time to think about it, his pocket vibrated.

He pulled his cell phone out. "Hello?"

"Uh, Brendan?" hiccuped Oscar. "I think I've made a

very important, if not odd, discovery."

"What are you looking at?" howled Colym from the top of his favorite sitting rock.

Oscar turned back to his phone. "I think I've either discovered Leprechauns or I discovered that I should never, ever drink."

Colym stood up and tried to shoo Oscar away. "Be gone with you, figment."

Oscar stared at the little green-clad fellow in absolute confusion. "I think I need help, Brendan."

Brendan chuckled. "Just find a nice spot to lay down and we'll be there in a little bit." He ended the call and laughed. "My dad is in Corways."

"Oh?" replied Dorian.

"Yeah, and I think he just met Colym." Brendan smiled.

Dorian had to smile back. "Then let's hurry so Colym doesn't ruin our reputation any more than he already has."

Riding on the griffin was a much different ride than with Gorgoch. It was the difference between a speedboat and a sailboat. Gorgoch was careful to not make anyone sick or to scare any of the passengers, but the griffin seemed to make that its priority. Thankfully, the beast's back was large enough to house all three of the full sized passengers and the two carry-ons.

Lizzie tried to peer through the wind to find out where they were, but even if she had been able to see anything, it was doubtful that she would have recognized any landmarks. So she decided to ask instead. "Are we there yet?"

Both Dorian and Brendan scowled at her and she chuckled. "Just kidding, but seriously, how long until we're there?"

Dorian had the best view since she was in the front. "Judging by the speed of our new friend, I'd say we'll be there in less than an hour.

True to her prediction, the griffin touched down in the center of Corways in fifty-three minutes. Of course, when it landed, the Leprechauns in town scattered and screamed and it was a scene of general terror, but after a little assurance from Dorian, the little people came out of hiding.

The griffin pawed the ground as if to say sorry.

"Dorian!" cooed the crowd. They shouted out greetings and good cheer, but inevitably someone asked about Duncan.

"He…" was all she managed to say.

Brendan held her hand and took it from there. "King Duncan died a hero."

Biddy stood proudly on the griffin's back. "It is a tale for another time, my friends."

Rory walked up behind her and put his arm around her shoulders. "Dorian is now queen." He struggled with his words and everyone in town knew why. Duncan had been loved, and he would be missed. "Please, allow us to settle in and there will be time to tell our adventure."

"Oh," remembered Lizzie. "Has anyone seen a tall human around here?" After a few smart alecks pointed at her, a few others pointed down the trail. "Thanks."

Dorian, Lizzie, and Brendan walked down the path until they came upon Colym's sitting rock. Colym wasn't currently perched on his rock in a drunken stupor. He was actually curled up next to Oscar beneath a tall, thick trunk in a drunken stupor.

"Colym, you lazy bum, get up and get into town," suggested Dorian.

The stereotypical Leprechaun roused and protested. "But why? This human is so warm, and he smells like my favorite drinks."

"Get moving."

"Fine." Colym got to his feet and staggered across Oscar's chest. He reached the end of Oscar and fell into a small growth of grass. A giant *Burp!* sounded from the patch, which was then followed by the distinct sound of snoring.

Dorian shrugged and Brendan leaned down and poked Oscar on the arm. "Wake up, Dad."

"Huh?" He smacked his lips with the thirsty sounds of waking from a nap.

"Come on, Dad, get up," prodded Lizzie.

Oscar opened one eye, feeling out the environment. "Brendan! Lizzie! It's you!" He tried to scramble to his feet but the pounding headache behind his eyes wouldn't allow that to happen.

"Easy now. I got you." Brendan put an arm under his dad's arm and hoisted him up.

Oscar noticed Dorian and smiled.

"Oh, Dad," began Brendan. "This is Dorian."

"She's his girlfriend," teased Lizzie. Both Dorian and Brendan blushed giving Lizzie great satisfaction.

"Shut up, Liz," Brendan replied playfully.

"It is a pleasure to meet you, young lady." Oscar shook Dorian's hand.

The O'Neals and Dorian took their time walking back to the village. Oscar went on and on about his crazy dream and Leprechauns—remembering nothing of his encounter in Wales or the fact that he had stowed the music box deep in his suitcase—but when they entered the town square he abruptly stopped talking.

"Are you seeing this, too?" he asked the others.

"Seeing what?" teased Lizzie again. Brendan shot her a sour look, but she kept the smile plastered on her face.

"The… the… the Leprechauns," Oscar shouted. The griffin spread its wings and stomped the ground. "And whatever that is!"

"Yes, Dad, we see them, too," Brendan said, assuring his father.

"Oh, okay. So this means?"

"Basically it means all that stuff that we think of as magic and myth are real," confirmed Lizzie. "Kind of freaky, huh?"

Oscar agreed and then asked for two aspirin and a glass of water.

✦ ✦ ✦

The Leprechauns were some sort of clan, thought Brendan. They had found the torn up little rental car and had magically mended it to its original crappy self. Magic could only do so much, it seemed. It was in that little car that Dorian drove the O'Neals to the airport.

Screeeech!

After sliding to a stop at the curb, Oscar threw his door open and bent down to put his head between his legs to keep from vomiting.

"Did I do something wrong?" Dorian smiled shyly.

"Nope, he's just fired up about how great of a driver you are," lied Brendan.

Oscar took the car and drove it around to the rental place and left instructions for the kids to meet him at Gate 4 in twenty minutes.

"Thanks for all your help, Lizzie."

Lizzie shook off the thanks. "It was my pleasure, Dorian. I learned a lot on this little trip."

"Do you think your dad was okay with what he found out about your ancestors?"

Brendan shrugged. "I think so. Just knowing that the O'Neals had lived in that area before they came to the States seemed to satisfy him." Brendan scratched his head. "Though, I'm a little disappointed that it turns out we aren't descended from Leprechauns."

"Well, you performed as admirably as any Leprechaun," smiled Dorian. "And besides, your clan worked side by side with my ancestors all throughout the Magick Wars, and you continued their legacy."

Lizzie looked up at the sight of a red sports car zooming their direction. "That's the chump who splashed us."

"Oh yeah." Brendan held out his palm and the front tire blew apart, sending the red car into a spin. It spun all the way into a small retention pond where the water was just up to the half way mark on the door. The sunglasses-wearing dude inside tried to wipe all the muck off his face.

"Cool," said Lizzie. "Hey, wait a minute. You get to have magic powers to take home? No fair!"

"I already told you, I'm cool like that," he smirked.

"Bye, Dorian." She hugged the Irish girl and stuck her tongue out at Brendan before walking away, talking to herself about how ridiculous it was that Brendan had magic and…

Dorian fixed Brendan with a stare. "Why is it that you still have your power long after the rest of us lost ours?"

"I don't know." He shrugged. The name Nauda ran through his mind. Morna had called him Nauda's champion, but he still didn't know the name, and he was too afraid to ask Dorian about it. He knew he had Google on his phone, and he told himself to take some time to learn all about this Nauda.

She stared at him again.

"Honest," he said holding up his hands to display his innocence. "Luck of the Irish, I suppose." He gave her his most charming smile. "Oh, thanks for hanging onto my sword for me. I don't think they would have let me on the plane with it."

"It will hold a place of honor in Corways, but," Dorian smirked in a sultry way. "I want you to take this back to America with you."

Brendan's heart leapt to his throat as Dorian wrapped her arms around his neck. He could barely breathe when she smiled and leaned in for a kiss that was truly magical.

Epilogue
✛ Old Things New ✛

THE DARKNESS HAD NOT LEFT the Black Forest with the demise of Morna. Instead, the storm had grown worse and the landscape more ominous. The trees grouped themselves together as if for some sort of protection. The wind was harsh and unrelenting. The clouds billowed overhead and the rain fell in sheets dropping black water on the landscape. The river threatened to overtake its banks.

Any creatures, predator and prey alike, were forced to run as the ground shook and sharp, jagged obsidian was forced upwards piercing the land. All over the Black Forest these rocks appeared and tore at unfortunate trees and stabbed into herds of animals. The death and destruction only fueled what came next.

Black lightning shot out of the sky and struck the tower of Morna's castle. The bolt entered through the balcony window and slammed into the dagger that pinned the witch's lifeless body to the altar. The dagger hummed and became heated. Morna's body burst into black flames that licked at the altar but could not burn it. It only took seconds for her corpse to char and turn ashen.

The storm raged on, but all seemed still within the tower. That was until the skeletal hand of a long forgotten evil cleaved its way through the middle of Morna's charred remains. It emerged up to the shoulder and the boney fingers found their hold on the handle of the dagger. Using the dagger for leverage, a skeleton dragged itself out of the altar and found its footing on the stone floor. Still clinging to the dagger, the skeleton took stock of its environment.

With a a wave of its hand Morna's ashes and the ashes of the insignificant Leprechaun king swirled through the air around it. The cloud of death encircled the skeleton and it held the dagger out, pointing it toward the balcony and the enraged sky. Black lightning struck the dagger again sending crackling streams of energy circulating throughout the ash dome.

The energy and ash crackled and baked and shrank in on the skeleton. Wet flesh and muscle began to take hold, sticking to the bones. More and more tissue affixed to the bone, splotchy and bleeding. Time sped and soon the entire frame was covered in new flesh and porcelain skin. Golden hair grew at an accelerated rate and fell upon the shoulder of the newly formed being. The rest of the ash took the forms of armor and a cape.

The being admired the new attire and the flowing cape and the black glint of his lightweight armor. He held the dagger out and it extended twelve inches to become a formidable sword. He sheathed it at his waist and walked toward the balcony. He paused near a wall and waved his palm over it. Instantly, a cloud of smoke seeped out from between the stones and came together in a kneeling mass at the feet of the golden haired being.

"Dullahan," the being said. "I call upon your service."

Dullahan made a fist and crossed his chest. "I pledge my service to you, my lord."

"Rise. There is much to do." The being and Dullahan stepped onto the balcony and looked out over the Black Forest at the wasteland that it had become. "Behold, my old friend. Elathan's kingdom upon this earth begins small and simple, but soon it will be as grand as my others."

"Yes, my lord," agreed Dullahan, standing at his new master's side.

✦ ✦ ✦

Somewhere over the Atlantic Ocean, a passenger plane

glided through the air at five hundred and seventy miles per hour on route to New York's La Guardia Airport. The flight attendant had just handed Brendan a bag of peanuts and a Coke when he felt it. He closed his eyes and shook his head.

"What's the matter?" asked Lizzie. "Feel a disturbance in the force?" she joked.

Brendan chuckled a little. "Something like that."

"What do you think it was?"

"I'm not sure." Brendan lowered his voice and leaned in to whisper to Lizzie. "Before the witch died, she warned me that I should get ready for war because some greater evil was on its way."

Lizzie just stared at him. "You mean this whole thing isn't over?"

Brendan didn't know how to answer. He leaned his head back and tried not to think about it, but he could feel that it wasn't over. He opened his bag of peanuts and took a swig from his Coke.

"I'm sure she was just talking, that's all." He smiled at his sister. "I'm sure it was nothing. I'm just tired."

Brendan looked down as they flew through the troposphere just above a bank of storm clouds. He was surprised at how strange it felt to actually be flying above the clouds like that and not be riding a ghost or a griffin. Brendan eyed the lightning carefully. Dark magic was coursing through the atmosphere ripping through the sky in black streaks. He heaved a heavy breath knowing that the lightning represented suffering and pain and things that were yet to come, but he couldn't bring himself to tell Lizzie about any of that.

On the other side of the aisle, Oscar clutched the Knot Charm in his hand and felt the comfort it offered him. It was warm and familiar. He thought that he might just toss it in a drawer when he got home, but he wasn't sure that was possible. It was too comforting to hold, and he recognized that he might be relying on it to some degree to help calm his nerves.

Luckily, his airplane seat was comfortable. He was so comfortable that the familiar presence of the shadowed man from his dream escaped him, even though the man who sat three rows back was one and the same.

The dark stranger projected his thought into Oscar's mind. "*Two sisters yet to find. Do not fail me.*"

"I won't fail," mumbled Oscar as he turned away.

Brendan glanced over at his father. He had sensed something odd about the old man since they met up in Corways, but he couldn't place what it was. At the time, he was just happy to see his father alive and well, but something about him was different. He recognized it now.

It could be nothing, he told himself, but the witch's warning had him on edge. He didn't know from which direction or in what form danger would come, but it didn't really matter, because Morna had been right about one thing. He was Nuada's champion, and that meant something great—or least he hoped it did.

✛ Celtic Mythos ✛
The Megalith Union

A Preview of Book 2 in the *Celtic Mythos* Series

Brad A. LaMar

Please note this is an uncorrected proof from the author's manuscript. Changes to the text may be made before publication. Please consult with the publisher before quoting from this text.

Prologue

✝ The First Wave ✝

The Cobb – 1721

How many people are with us, Da?"

His daughter's voice pulled Toren O'Neal from his thoughts as he tilted his head in her direction. He smiled an old man's smile though he was only five and forty years.

"I don't know, Sorcha." He stroked his young daughter's hair and held her closer. "So many want what we want."

"A better life?" Sorcha replied.

"Aye, a better life in America."

Toren had found a small place for himself and his daughter in the hold of the large British ship, The Cobb. They were joined by families that numbered in the hundreds: Scots, Irish, and Brits alike, all destined for America. Many believed that the young British colony was their best chance at having a life they could call their own. Perhaps a life that was joyous.

That was not why Toren O'Neal had joined the voyage, however. That was not why he had uprooted his precious

Sorcha from his family land in Ireland. He glanced down at his daughter and was comforted that she had fallen asleep, her breath in sync with the rhythmic motion of the ship on the water. He closed his own eyes and fell back into his memory.

✦ ✦ ✦

How many weeks had it been since he had last left Corways? As much as he loved the town and her people, leaving had not been a difficult decision. However, as it always is where close communities are concerned, he felt guilty for leaving. Queen Finna had tried her best to convince him to stay.

"I still don't understand why you think you need to leave, Toren," stated the miniscule queen, looking agitated and exasperated.

Toren had known Queen Finna and her clan for his entire life. Generations had passed and their lands had sat side by side with nary an argument to be had. The O'Neal clan and the village of Corways lived as true neighbors, looking out for the other and counting on the other to do the same.

"I know it is hard to understand, but it is in everyone's best interest that I take Sorcha and go."

Queen Finna was elegant royalty and was a good and fair leader. She had shimmering silver hair that was tied neatly in a bun and sat just below her crown. Her blue dress casually danced on the breeze. Her Leprechaun clan, as they referred to themselves, had thrived for thousands of years with very little contact with humans.

The O'Neal clan was the exception.

"There's nothing that can be done about it, Finna," Toren continued. "Fate has forced my decision and I have no choice."

"Why don't you have a choice?" Queen Finna willed herself to take full human size. Normally, this would have fascinated a person, but Toren had already seen it happen dozens of times. She stepped closer and reached for his hand in a grandmotherly manner. "Your family has been as close to our village as any family of Leprechauns. I don't see why you would need to go."

Toren patted Finna's hand and sighed. "My father made me promise to do all that's within my power to protect Corways and her people. This is something I have to do."

Finna was speechless, and he recognized her silence for trust. She trusted that he was making the right decision, but as he sat in the hold of The Cobb gliding to an uncertain future, he wasn't sure if he trusted his own judgment.

He shook off the doubt as he looked at his Sorcha's innocent face. To keep her innocent and to protect her was his task, and in America he would find a way.

✦ ✦ ✦

"Conchar," whispered a voice in the wizard's head.

Conchar had grown used to the voice and by all accounts wanted to ignore it, but it was persistent and unshakable. He had reluctantly begun following the voice's commands and fulfilling its requests. Requests like standing on a little plot of land adjacent to Corways. This was a dangerous place to stand considering that the war with the Leprechauns was ongoing.

"Why have you brought me here?" Conchar demanded.

The voice remained silent. Conchar knew from experience that the voice would continue speaking when it chose to, so he began to walk the grounds. Being a wizard, he already had acute senses when it came to the arcane, but since the voice had joined him no more than eleven months prior, his senses had become exponentially better. This enhanced sensory perception easily picked up the powerful, latent energy that permeated the land. Conchar doubted that he needed the enhancement from the voice to sense the power this land held. Admittedly, he might have mistaken the sensation for something else entirely, but he would have sensed it nonetheless.

He walked the lush, green acreage pressing his boot heals into the ground with each step. He took his time and was careful to search high and low all across the landscape. He was a keen observer, but noticed little that was out of the ordinary. Trees, acres of crops, a shed, a small cottage were all there was. He halted his stride when he reached the threshold of the cottage.

"Go in," commanded the voice.

Conchar obeyed and pushed the door open. It swung inwards without resistance, and he stepped inside. His eyes were overcome by the darkness, but he willed his vision to compensate, and the entirety of the room soon came into view. There was nothing fancy about the amenities in this home, not like his castle in the Black Forrest in Scotland. The family that lived here were not poor by Irish standards, but they were not affluent either.

"Who lived here?" he asked the voice.

No reply.

Conchar took note of the haphazard surroundings and deduced that they family left in haste. Why they ran, he was sure only the voice and the family knew.

"It is not here," sighed the voice.

"What is not here?"

The voice paused. "It matters not currently. Come. We have much to do in preparation of my return."

This statement took Conchar by surprise. "Your return? Who says that I would allow that?"

The voice actually chuckled. "It is incredible that you think you have a choice. To be clear, you are marked as mine, and to be in my favor will hold great rewards."

Greed was deep within Conchar's heart and he could not conceal his pleasure.

"Come," repeated the voice. "Your master commands it."

Conchar strode to the door and into the night air. "And what name does my master answer to?"

"You may address me as Elathan."

Conchar smirked with satisfaction as the clouds burst open and showered the earth with rain. Black lightning flashed across the sky and Conchar knew that he was in the favor of gods.

✛ About The Author ✛

When he's not fighting evil witches and wizards, Brad A. LaMar is an educator who resides in the Indianapolis Metropolitan area. He has taught science to middle school students for twelve years and works with teachers facilitating professional development and school improvement. He is married to Lori, a beautiful and supportive woman, and together they're raising Evan and Paige, two intelligent and wonderful children.

The idea for the *Celtic Mythos* series came from his love of science fiction and fantasy and the underutilized and abundantly rich folklore of the Celtic people. They are so much more than Leprechauns! Brad has always loved a good story, and upon researching the mythos of the Celtic Isles he became enthralled in the type of story he could tell.

Brad has always enjoyed writing, but in the beginning it was more for examples to share with his students than it was for anything else. It wasn't long before Brad found himself writing every night and submitting his work for publication. Brad finds publishing a tedious and painstaking process, but he says it's worth it. There are so many more stories to tell, and he can't wait to get started.

CPSIA information can be obtained
at www.ICGtesting.com
Printed in the USA
FFOW03n1131260115
10555FF